KV-683-282

ANGELS WITHOUT WINGS

Cavan County Library
Withdrawn Stock

Mark O'Sullivan is the acclaimed and award-winning author of the bestselling *Melody for Nora* (winner of the 1995 Bisto Book Eilís Dillon Memorial Award, shortlisted for the 1995 Reading Association of Ireland Award, winner of a White Raven Award – international librarians' award; *Wash-Basin Street Blues*, also a bestseller; *More than a Mulch* and *White Lies* (all published by Wolfhound Press). *Angels Without Wings* is one of his latest books. Mark lives in Thurles with his wife and daughters and works in Cashel, County Tipperary.

To Statia
And for Peter in memory

REVIEWS

ANGELS WITHOUT WINGS
'I could barely put it down.' *14-year-old reviewer*

MELODY FOR NORA
Winner of Eilís Dillon Memorial Award
White Raven award-winner
Short-listed for the Reading Association of Ireland Award

'A gripping storyline.' *Irish Times*

'Fast-moving and exciting.' *Books Ireland*

WASH-BASIN STREET BLUES
'O'Sullivan tells this tale of murder and mystery straight, keeping the tension between good and evil deliciously sustained.' *Irish Times*

MORE THAN A MATCH
'An excellent writer who displays a humane understanding of well-established characters in a story that engages sentimental concern.' *Irish Times*

ANGELS WITHOUT WINGS

MARK O'SULLIVAN

WOLFHOUND PRESS

CAVAN COUNTY LIBRARY
ACC. No. C109128
CLASS No. J (MD)
INVOICE NO. 4720 IES
PRICE £3.84

First published 1997 by
WOLFHOUND PRESS Ltd
68 Mountjoy Square
Dublin 1

© 1997 Mark O'Sullivan

All rights reserved. No part of this book may be reproduced or utilised in any form or by any means electronic or mechanical including photography, filming, recording, video recording, photocopying, or by any information storage and retrieval system or shall not, by way of trade or otherwise, be lent, resold or otherwise circulated in any form of binding or cover other than that in which it is published without prior permission in writing from the publisher.

This book is fiction. All characters, incidents and names have no connection with any persons living or dead. Any apparent resemblance is purely coincidental.

Wolfhound Press receives financial assistance from the Arts Council/
An Chomhairle Ealaíon, Dublin.

British Library Cataloguing in Publication Data
A catalogue record for this book is available from the British Library.

ISBN 0-86327-591-5

Cover photographs: Bottom courtesy David Davison & E. E. O'Donnell, from the Father Browne Collection.
Cover design: Slick Fish Design, Dublin
Typesetting: Wolfhound Press
Printed and bound by The Guernsey Press Co. Ltd, Guernsey, Channel Islands

CONTENTS

'Just as God creates angels, the writer creates characters. But these are angels without wings. Only the reader, by the power of imagination, can give them the wings to fly.'

Axel Hoffen

PROLOGUE

Red flames licked the night sky over Berlin. The covers, the pages, the words of twenty thousand books fuelled a vast bonfire. Smoke billowed across ranks of torch-bearing students and uniformed men. The deep sucking roar of the flames was like a vast collective gasp. It was as if those who were gathered there had, all at once, stopped to consider the horror of what they were witnessing.

Then a lone voice screamed out a defiant cry of 'Heil Hitler'. It was more than just a cry of praise for the Führer. It was a cry that said, 'We don't care what the world thinks of us.' 'Heil Hitler!' the crowd repeated time after time. The words echoed across the city, across Germany, across the entire continent of Europe and beyond. The message was clear. 'Those who are not with us are against us — and we will burn their every word!'

On that night of May 10th 1933, Axel Hoffen stood among the onlookers massed behind the throng of students near the University. He was a small, insignificant-looking man of thirty-two with thinning hair and gaunt, unshaven cheeks. Like most writers, he went unrecognised on the streets and tonight he had reason to be glad of that. If it had been known that his books were among those on the pyramid of fire he would certainly have been set upon there and then. The deep sense of foreboding he felt was briefly relieved by an excited pride. His books were being destroyed along with those of Europe's finest writers and thinkers: Thomas Mann, Stefan Zweig, Albert Einstein, H.G. Wells ... The feeling that he'd taken his place among the greats almost brought a smile to his face. But even a smile would have been dangerous. These people were deadly serious. Their voices left Axel in no doubt as to what would follow this night: a persecution without end — or rather, a persecution with an end that was unthinkable.

The intense heat of the bonfire and of the crowd pressing close against him had Axel in a lather of sweat. Blinded by his misted-over glasses, he stumbled through the crowd. Along the wide avenue of Unter Den Linden he half-walked, half-ran as though they were already in pursuit of him. But he was alone, quite alone. He stopped and leaned against a tall linden tree to catch his breath and gather his confused thoughts. There was only one place he could go, one person he could turn to, the only friend he had left in all of Berlin. His publisher, Herr Stieglitz.

It was six years now since Axel had first trudged dismally up that rickety flight of stairs to Herr Stieglitz's office. He'd done the rounds of publishers with his first collection of poems, *Night Songs*, and met only rejection. Within five minutes, the large, bearded man had simply said, 'Yes.' Axel floated on a silver-lined cloud all the way to that wonderful day of publication. His first book, his name along the cloth-bound spine of a real book! And then he waited. And waited.

Nothing happened. No one bought the book — no one, at least, besides his family back in distant Austadt. Axel was devastated; and worse, he was hungry too. There was no work to be had in Berlin and he was too proud to return home. But somehow he persisted. He wrote another book of poems, *Mist and Light*, and brought them to Herr Stieglitz. Axel was stunned by the man's reaction.

'These are difficult times ....', Herr Stieglitz began.

'But you haven't even read them.'

'We have to face reality, Axel ....'

'To hell with reality!'

Axel was, of course, as aware as everyone else of the reality of the times. In the last few years Germany had been on the slide and poverty was rife, nowhere more so than in Berlin. Life had become a matter of survival from one day to the next. Soon Herr Stieglitz had convinced Axel of what he must do to survive.

Besides publishing poetry, Herr Stieglitz also produced books for young people. The profits from these adventure stories allowed him to get unknown poets like Axel into print. Poetry was Herr Stieglitz's first love, but there was no profit in that business — as Axel had learned to his cost.

'It's as simple as this, Axel,' Herr Stieglitz told him. 'If you could write some stories for me then I could publish your poems.'

'You want me to write adventures! I'm a poet, for heaven's sake!'

'And very soon you'll be a dead poet.'

'But I've never done anything like this before. I wouldn't know how....'

'You're a *writer*, Axel. You were young once — why, compared to me you're still just a lad. What more do you need to dream up a story?'

Axel set to work reluctantly and came up with *The Adventures of the Lingen Gang*. Neither he nor Herr Stieglitz could have anticipated the huge popularity of the book. *The Lingen Gang and the Missing Bicycles* and *The Lingen Gang and the Lost Boy* soon followed. Axel no longer starved but, at first, he took litle pleasure from his new prosperity.

Always, there was this niggling sense of failure. He hadn't become the respected poet he had once dreamed of being. His second collection of poems had sold even fewer copies than the first. So, from time to time, he would try to be a poet again.

However, each time he sat before the typewriter and the bundle of blank pages, his mind was filled, not with the airy stuff of verse, but with the words and deeds of his four young adventurers. When Axel touched the typewriter keys he felt as though he were descending into a trance that drew him hypnotically to that imagined world of adventure. He cursed the Gang, raged against their strange hold over him, blamed them for destroying the poetry in his mind. And then the unexpected came along again to surprise him.

Axel discovered that when he stopped being angry with himself and with the Gang, he actually enjoyed writing these stories. He came to feel a growing affection for the characters he had created. Sometimes, as he lay in that suspended state between waking and sleeping, he actually thought of them as being real. He knew exactly what Siegfried and Dieter, Anna and Greta looked like. In his mind's eye was a perfectly clear picture, almost like a photograph, of the mountain village of Leiningen in which they lived.

He began to wonder whether Herr Stieglitz might not have been right when he'd once said, 'I think you've found your life's work, Axel. Your future is secure, and how many men can say that?'

Then, shortly before this night of the burning books, Adolf Hitler came to power. Axel's future no longer brimmed with promise. The new Nazi-controlled government moved quickly to silence those whose ideas were different from its own. Writers were among the first to be regarded with suspicion.

In Axel's case it was that first collection of poems that drew the attention of the Nazis. Its message of peace and tolerance displeased them. *Night Songs* was banned. *Mist and Light* soon followed onto the blacklist, as did the three Lingen Gang adventures.

Perhaps if the Gang had included only Siegfried and Greta, the perfect German boy and girl — the one handsome, the other beautiful — then the books might have gone unnoticed. However, there was also Anna, who was Jewish, and Dieter, a boy born with one arm. That these four should get along so well together and show such trust and loyalty towards one another was simply unacceptable to those who now ruled in Germany. For them, the Jew was the enemy; the 'cripple', a mere burden on society.

Herr Stieglitz no longer fitted his over-sized clothes very well. Axel sat down before him and wiped the moisture from his glasses in disbelief. All about him books and papers, many of them torn to shreds, lay scattered around the floor. The laughter lines on the large man's face had turned to furrows of worry that were stained red with blood and purple with bruises.

'They've been here,' Herr Stieglitz sighed. 'They've closed us down. Stieglitz Press doesn't exist any more.'

He was, he explained, penniless now. The bank in which he'd deposited his money for years had refused to hand over even one mark of what was rightfully his.

'I've got just about enough money to get to America, Axel. My advice to you is to do the same. Go to your bank tomorrow, before it's too late.'

There was a terrible finality about their parting handshake and Axel couldn't quite believe Herr Stieglitz's reassuring words.

'In America we will meet again. In America we will start all over again. You'll see.'

Next morning Axel went to the bank. The outcome was predictable.

'Your finances are being investigated by the authorities,' the small, balding clerk sporting a little Hitler moustache smiled.

A copper name-plate set grandly on the polished timber counter read 'Herr Gier'.

Later that same evening Axel followed the bank clerk to his home. Away from the gaze of his manager, he imagined, this Herr Gier might prove to be more sympathetic. Axel couldn't have been more wrong.

'Get out of here,' the man warned, his apartment door open no more than a few inches.

'All I need is enough money to leave Germany. I'll never bother you, ever again.'

'If you haven't gone in ten seconds I'll ring some of my friends in the Brownshirts.'

It came as no surprise to Axel to hear that Herr Gier was a member of that bullying troop of henchmen, the SA, who were as cruel as they were blind in their devotion to Adolf Hitler. Beyond the clerk he saw a table strewn with bank-notes. He looked again at those piggish eyes.

'That's my money, isn't it?'

'I'm picking up the phone right now.'

'The police will hear of this.'

'And you think they'll believe an enemy of the Führer? Don't make me laugh.'

He slammed the door in Axel's face.

Now Axel lived in real fear of the knock on the attic door that would spell arrest and consignment to a concentration camp or, worse still, to the secret torture chambers of the black-uniformed SS or the brown-shirted SA. The rumours spreading around Berlin about these places instilled terror in the bravest of souls.

His *Night Songs* became the whimpers of a broken man in a darkness filled with heavy, doom-laden footsteps and conspiratorial whispers on the stairway leading to his room.

The silence which had descended on his young characters was even more complete. In that grey room somewhere in the back of Axel's mind they waited, forgotten by the world, forgotten even by Axel himself. Until that fateful knock came on the attic door on an April night in 1934 and a man in black SS uniform burst into Axel's life with an incredible proposal.

And the Lingen Gang's leader slowly woke from his sleep to begin the most daring adventure of all — an adventure that would take him and his companions from the pleasant, fictional heights of their mountain village to the grim reality of Berlin; from the little complications of everyday life in Leiningen to the horror of a country in the grip of Nazism; from the despairing mind of a young writer to an all-too-real and dangerous existence in the outside world.

The attic door rattles. Axel trembles. In the Grey Room of his dulled imaginings a new life beyond his control begins.

THE GREY ROOM

Siegfried was the first to stir as if he were a real boy roused from an ordinary sleep. When he woke, however, he was himself a creature of dream. Ghost-like, a pencil-sketch figure, he was as grey as the room in which he and the other Gang members sat. The table before them with its vase of white flowers; the chairs where they sat, one to each of its four sides; the two stone archways at opposite ends of the room, covered with makeshift curtains; the very bodies of the Lingen Gang — all were as light and insubstantial as old cobwebs.

No breeze rustled through the room, no sound intruded. And, for a while, no thoughts intruded on the blank spaces of Siegfried's mind. His mind was not yet his own, and he had no inkling of the subtle change in the dry air around him. The room was getting colder, the atmosphere tense with foreboding. Something crackled through his grey limbs like a light frost on a bare winter branch. Along the delicate strands of his spine it went, and on into the mesh of spindly fibres that was his brain

This cold feeling of dread was the first true emotion Siegfried had ever felt. His eyelids, slight as insect wings, trembled and the trembling spread like a fire of ice. Then, all at once, his mind exploded into being.

Reeling back in his chair from the panic of memories and the loud, inexplicable knocking that rushed through him, he reached out to keep himself from falling. His hand passed through the sapless table but he struggled to his feet. Behind him, the chair tumbled to the floor and lost its shape in a cloud of dust. He looked at the others, but none of them had moved so much as a feathery eyelash.

Slowly, the barrage of unconnected thoughts eased and he began to make sense of them. Words formed in his mind and he was startled to find the same words break from his parched lips into the silence. Even as he spoke, he knew that a man called Axel Hoffen was his maker but that these words were his own.

'My name is Siegfried Geistengel. I'm fourteen years old. I live in the village of Leiningen. These are my friends, Anna, Dieter and Greta. We're the Lingen Gang.'

The relentless banging noise accompanied his every thought. As the brave, manly hero of the Lingen Gang adventures Siegfried had never known fear. Now, everything frightened him: this grey room, the absolute stillness of his companions, the knocking inside of him.

He began to move cautiously about the room, fearful that he might crumble apart as the chair had. Everything in the room was familiar to him — except that the colours were missing. The books on the little set of shelves were no longer red, yellow, green, blue as he remembered them. His treasured trinket box had lost its golden sheen. The posters of Max Schmeling, the famous German heavyweight boxer, and Lilian Harvey, the actress, had changed to black and white.

Suddenly, his attention was drawn from these grey copies of the Gang room's contents. He had recognised that dull thumping sound.

'My heart! It's my heartbeat!'

No sooner had he realised this than a more urgent rapping caught his ear. It was only then that he noticed the archways at either end of the room. The noise was coming from the one to his left.

The sense of dread thickened with every step he took towards that archway. Somehow he knew who it was he would meet there: Axel Hoffen, his creator. He knew too that he had been born of the fear which leaked out of that man's room to this grey one.

Within feet of the archway he hesitated. A new and astonishing thought had burst upon his mind.

'If I can think for myself then I'm becoming real ... a real person!'

Siegfried braced himself and stepped over the threshold into the dingy attic room of reality.

Axel Hoffen lay on his bed, whimpering quietly and staring in terror at the splintering woodwork of the door opposite where Siegfried had entered. When Axel turned towards Siegfried he saw nothing, at first, but a blank wall. Then the door behind him burst open and on the wall, precisely where Siegfried was standing, appeared the giant shadow of a soldier and the gross, exaggerated shape of a gun.

Axel wheeled around and raised himself from his crouched position on the bed. His eyes met the cold blue discs beneath the creased brows of a fair-haired man in the doorway.

Siegfried's eyes were fixed on Axel. Could this weeping, pitiful man really be his creator? Siegfried gaped at the lank black thatch of unwashed hair, the dishevelled clothes, the tattered shoes. He grimaced at Axel's craven words, spoken in the tremulous voice of a frightened old lady.

'I'm so sorry. You see, I sleep too soundly and I imagined I was dreaming and that ...'

The man advanced into the attic room and Siegfried could see him more clearly. Below the black peaked hat was a face carved as if from granite: pale, square-jawed, with high cheekbones. His uniform was black. The collar was aluminium-edged; on its left side were two silvery flashes of wire; on its right, three bright four-cornered stars. A silver strap glistened on his right shoulder. His tall boots were mirror-black.

'Ah, you were sleeping. Or perhaps you were simply trying to hide something? Have you been writing more of that pernicious filth of yours?'

Siegfried looked in disgust from Axel to his tormentor. If this had been a Lingen Gang story he would have sprung immediately to the rescue of the victim; but now that he had a mind of his own, he felt no pity for the sobbing wreck on the bed.

'This ... this miserable creature made me!' he cried out in disbelief, but neither Axel nor the man in uniform heard him.

'I've written nothing. Not since ... so long I can't remember. You know I haven't — and even if I had, who'd publish it anyway, Lieutenant?'

'Captain, actually. SS Haupsturmführer Teufel, to be precise.'

He took a seat by an old second-hand table on which stood the typewriter which had given birth to the Lingen Gang three years before. He removed his hat and placed it lovingly on the table.

'If it hadn't been for your Jewish friend Stieglitz, none of that nonsense you wrote would have seen the light of day. But where are your Jewish friends now, eh, when you need them?'

'I *have* no Jewish friends.'

Siegfried, remembering his friend Anna, was shocked by the venom of Axel's words.

'Perhaps, perhaps not. But soon none of you people will have any Jewish friends and we shall have no Jewish enemies.'

Teufel smashed out some keys on the rusted typewriter without once taking his attention from Axel.

'What about cripples? This imbecile Dieter in your books would seem to suggest you have a certain, how shall I put it, a certain sympathy for these inferior beings. You like cripples?'

Axel squirmed beneath the Haupsturmführer's persistent gaze.

'No,' he whispered, crossing his arms over his chest.

'I can't hear you, Hoffen.'

Axel shrank wearily down, his body seeming to fold in on itself. Teufel peeled off his black leather gloves and placed them beside his hat on the table. On his right hand a silver ring in the shape of a skull and crossbones caught the weak stream of light from the outside landing. He stood, tall in his meticulously polished boots, and advanced on Axel.

'Must I repeat myself, Hoffen? I can't hear you. Would you like to answer me?'

Axel's head moved from side to side and Teufel spoke again with a deliberate slowness, as if he were addressing a child or a foreigner.

'Does that mean no, you won't answer, or no, you don't like cripples?'

Siegfried felt a huge surge of hope as Axel drew himself up. The face seemed less panic-stricken; it gave the fleeting appearance of courage regained.

'It means ...' Axel began boldly, but Teufel's fist crushed into his mouth and sent him sprawling back on the bed.

Siegfried charged at Teufel but his flailing arms did no more than ruffle the Haupsturmführer's blond hair. The man in black looked back briefly at the door, as though explaining to himself the breeze that had seemed to brush by his ear.

'Thank me!'

Axel glanced up in fearful puzzlement and spoke too urgently so as to avoid another blow.

'Tha ... thank ... thank you.'

Teufel sat alongside Axel on the bed and allowed the tautness of his hard jaw to mellow into something that was meant to resemble a smile.

'Why are you thanking me?'

'Because if I don't, you'll hit me again.'

'True enough. But there's something else. You see, Hoffen, I've come here to offer you a second chance.'

As helpless as Axel, Siegfried could only listen.

'You would like to redeem yourself in the eyes of our great Fuhrer? Yes?'

'Of course,' Axel muttered through swollen lips.

'Very well then. It comes down to this, Hoffen. You are to write another of these Lingen Gang stories, but this time you will do so on our terms. Your message will, as it were, coincide with ours.'

'But how?'

'It's quite simple. You see, Anna the Jewess and Dieter the cripple we do not approve of. You have made these degenerates the friends of good German types like Siegfried and Greta. You have made such friendships seem acceptable to many young people. It is time that this damage was undone.'

Siegfried couldn't understand why it was that Anna and Dieter were not approved of. And 'degenerates'? What did that mean?

'There will be no more sweet Jews or loyal cripples.'

'You want me to write a Lingen Gang book without Anna or Dieter?'

Teufel got up from the bed and began to pace the small room.

'That would be too easy. So easy as not to be worth the trouble. No, what we have in mind is for the treachery of the Jew and the uselessness of the cripple, for these facts to be made clear in the young readers' minds.'

He swung around and faced Axel.

'Do you understand?'

'Yes.'

Siegfried hadn't understood. The look of submission on Axel's bloodied face was, however, easier to comprehend. Moving lightly, the invisible boy walked to his creator's side. Without any real hope of having any effect, he touched Axel's cold forehead and whispered, 'You mustn't do it. Whatever it is this fellow wants you to do, you mustn't do it.'

Raising himself to his full height, Axel faced the imposing figure of Teufel. He breathed in deeply and spoke with a confidence that surprised even Siegfried.

'I understand. But I won't do it. There's too much twisting of young people's minds already in this country.'

Teufel, bewildered by the sudden change in Axel, prepared his fists for another assault.

'You've burned my books. No one reads them any more. Isn't that enough?'

'Wagner! Kroll!' Teufel called over his shoulder. 'Take this piece of scum to Headquarters!'

Two large, blocky men dressed in the same forbidding black charged through the doorway and took hold of Axel. Teufel had regained his composure. With an amused tilt of his head he told Axel, 'As it happens, your refusal makes little difference. You see, we had already made alternative arrangements in the event of your being unhelpful.'

Axel strained hopelessly between his arm-twisting captors.

'In precisely ten minutes, while you are enjoying our hospitality at Headquarters, I will be speaking to a certain, let us say, more willing writer. This very night he'll begin this Lingen Gang book. And the book will appear under your name. You will agree to this in time. Wagner and I can be quite persuasive when we need to be.'

'Why does it matter whether I agree or not?' Axel dared to ask. 'You'll put my name on it anyway, won't you?'

'It matters, my dear Hoffen, because your books are well known throughout Europe. I want you out there signing copies of this book and talking to those young people whose minds you've infected with your drivel. I want you to tell them that you've seen the error of your ways. You will travel from school to school and to Hitler Youth meetings, under our direction, of course. You will tell them the truth about the Jew and the cripple. Doesn't the prospect of all that travel, all that freedom, excite you, Hoffen?'

'Not particularly.'

Teufel beckoned to his henchmen.

'Take him from my sight. And Wagner?'

'Yes, Herr Haupsturmführer?'

'Try not to be too polite with Herr Hoffen.'

The bull-necked Wagner rubbed his hand over his close-shaven head. He grinned and pushed Axel towards the door. Siegfried's desperate attempts to release Axel proved futile. His powerless punches swept through the black cloth of their uniforms as they dragged the bleeding writer to the doorway and beyond. Teufel followed, replacing his hat and gloves. With one last contemptuous look around the attic room, he too was gone.

Standing among the debris of the smashed-in door, Siegfried was afraid to go further out. 'This very night', a new but unwelcome adventure was to begin in that other, safer world of Leiningen. But even Leiningen was hardly safe now. What fearful things would this 'more willing writer' force him and the other Gang members to do? And what was to become of Axel?

Siegfried retreated towards the Grey Room, his spirits only briefly brightened by the possibility that his companions might have woken too. But when he passed back into that silent, twilight place, Greta, Anna and Dieter sat just as he had left them.

Huddled in a corner of the room, Siegfried was already tired of thinking and shattered by this complete powerlessness that was so different from the strength that was his in the books. Time had never had any meaning for him before. In the stories, whole hours, sometimes days and weeks, went missing but neither he nor the others would ever have noticed. And the time spent resting in this Grey Room might have been a year or two or hundreds of years for all he knew.

Now, however, Siegfried was aware of the slow passage of time because he was alive to every minute, every plodding second of it. He would not, he realised, be fourteen forever any more. He would grow old. And then?

Suddenly, the sound he'd been waiting for — though he didn't realise it until it came — began to thrash out the ever-quickening seconds. It was the distant click-clacking of a typewriter. Somewhere out in that evil world of reality, a 'more willing writer' had begun his despicable task.

Siegfried found himself on his feet. At first, his mind protested at being summoned to the imaginary village. Walking, as if in a trance, to the second of those grey archways, he saw that it was best to follow the typewriter's beckoning. Leiningen was a more comfortable place to be; and if he was so easily drawn into it, then perhaps he wasn't becoming real after all. There, at least, he wouldn't have to think these disturbing thoughts.

As he gradually lost control of his own thoughts he saw the others rise from their chairs and move to the Leiningen archway. He called their names and with each name his mind emptied a little more. 'Anna, Dieter, Greta ...'

The mould-grey curtain opened. The blinding sunshine of Leiningen burned his brain into darkness and the fourth adventure of the Lingen Gang began.

THE LAST
OF THE
LINGEN GANG

PART 1

Siegfried Geistengel stands on the tumbledown parapet above the ruins of Leiningen Castle. A warm summer breeze tosses his mane of fair hair. His freckled forehead wrinkles anxiously as he watches the narrow path between the trees below. The meeting of the Lingen Gang should have started five minutes ago. Anna and Dieter are late again. Siegfried wonders if either of them takes their gang duties seriously any more.

He climbs down gingerly from the precariously high wall which is held together by a thick mantle of ivy. Once below, he descends a set of steps in the Castle floor. These moss-covered granite chunks lead to the maze of old wine cellars where the Gang room is located. At the bottom of these steps is a corbelled stone archway marking the entrance into the main wine cellar. A curtain made of old grain sacks deflects the breeze that too often sweeps down the stairwell. This room has been neatly disguised as the Gang room. With its table and chairs and wall posters, it appears to be in constant use.

However, behind a second patched-together curtain stands another archway and this conceals the real Gang room. This was Siegfried's idea. It was meant to fool those other gangs who, in the past, often attacked the Lingen Gang camp.

It has been a long time since the last attack. In fact, since the coming of our noble Fuhrer, Adolf Hitler, the energies of all the village gangs have been directed to more useful and grander purposes. All except the Lingen Gang. The boys of the village are now members of the splendid Hitler Youth. The girls are whole-heartedly devoted to the excellent League of German Girls. No longer do they behave like savage, competing tribes in some African jungle. Instead, a new spirit of orderliness and dedication to the Fatherland prevails. There is no escaping the fact that this is for the best.

As Siegfried walks through the main cellar it is quite clear to him that the Lingen Gang continues to exist only because of his own sense of loyalty to the others. Anna, the Jew, and Dieter, the one-armed cripple, would never be accepted by these new youth organisations. This is perfectly reasonable. After all, the Jews are responsible for so much that has gone wrong in Germany. As for Dieter, he can never be a fighter and Germany will need to fight to regain its rightful place in the world.

And yet, though his loyalty to this pair is being sorely tested of late, he is still too blinded by foolish sympathy to do what he so dearly wishes to do.

Every night as he waits to fall asleep he imagines himself in that proud light-brown uniform. More than that, he sees himself in the still finer uniform of Local Leader of the Leiningen Hitler Youth. This, the most eagerly sought-after rank, hasn't yet been filled but soon will be. But Anna's darkly pretty face and Dieter's mumblings always spoil the dream for him.

Siegfried pulls back the hemp curtain. Inside, Greta, with her flaxen hair tied up in smart coils, sits at the table in the centre of the room, concentrating fixedly on her report for the delayed meeting. Greta is an efficient secretary and tireless in every task she takes on. She is, too, a sensitive girl and a good judge of Siegfried's moods. As soon as he enters she is aware of his frustration and disappointment.

'They won't be long now,' she says, by way of consolation.

Siegfried sits heavily into his dark-timbered chair.

'Sometimes I wonder if there's any point in all of this. After what happened in the village yesterday I feel I must do something to protect our Fatherland. How can I do anything with a gang that's, wel .... only half a gang?'

'Perhaps it's time to ... to make a change?'

He shakes his head, not in refusal to consider the possibility but in genuine confusion. The events of the previous day flood his mind with waves of doubt, puzzlement and, above all, anger.

The new Village Hall in Leiningen was the first great achievement of the Local Council under the new National Socialist leadership of Herr Hempel, who is also Stationmaster at the village Railway Station. Under his benign but firm control the many unemployed men of the village and surrounding areas, grateful to have work to support their families, laboured stubbornly beneath rain and blistering sun. In two short months they built a fine two-storeyed affair, painted it a gleaming white and latticed its walls with spliced wood beams.

Now, Leiningen's first monument to National Socialism is charred and gutted. Siegfried, his head bowed at the Gang room table, remembers the scene he stumbled on the previous day.

Strong-armed labourers stood staring, their strength momentarily sapped by shock. Members of the local Brownshirt unit, the SA, searched among the rubble for what could be saved. Herr Stiefel, the baker, his clay-brown shirt smeared with grey ash, wept bitterly as he unearthed the scorched portrait of Adolf Hitler.

'They cannot destroy him!' he cried. 'See, his face is unblemished. They cannot destroy him!'

To his side came Herr Hempel, vaulting across broken beams; collarless, his sleeves rolled up determinedly.

'Tomorrow, we begin again,' he told Herr Stiefel — and then, as though suddenly inspired, added, 'No. Today. This very day. This very hour.'

He turned to the group of labourers and Brownshirts drawn towards him by his dogged air of resolve.

'Are you with me?' he bellowed. 'Are you with the Führer, Adolf Hitler?'

The roar that arose was spine-tingling after their stunned silence. A little knot of Hitler Youths had gathered, and they joined in the response to Herr Hempel's repeated call.

'Heil....'

'Hitler!'

'Heil....'

'Hitler!'

'Heil....'

'Hitler!'

The Village Hall was a hive of joyful activity within minutes. Close to where Siegfried stood, Herr Hempel spoke quietly to the youths in uniform.

'Your task,' he said, 'will be to work alongside the men and to find, if you can, some evidence of how this fire was started. Only then will we discover the filth who perpetrated this ... this desecration.'

'But we know who did it,' Herr Stiefel exclaimed as he passed by, shouldering an enormous charred beam. 'The Communists, the Jews. Dammit, they're all Jews, you know that as well as I do.'

He began to list off the names of those villagers he suspected. Siegfried wasn't surprised to hear that of Anna's father, the leader of the twenty or so Jews in Leiningen. Karl Matthias was not only a Jew but also a well-known Communist, which made him doubly suspect.

'We should thrash every last stinking one of them,' the baker insisted. 'We should burn them out of ...'

Herr Hempel placed his big soot-stained hand on Herr Stiefel's shoulder.

'First, we must find the evidence,' he said. 'And there *will* be evidence; because, you see, these people, for all their stealth, are basically fools. When we discover who is responsible, I can promise you that our revenge will be terrible.'

Before he reached Herr Hempel, Siegfried was already speaking in a mad rush of words and trying desperately to silence the voice of self-disgust in him.

'I want to help,' he pleaded. 'I have to. It's my duty, and I'm good at searching for clues and things and ...'

Herr Hempel listened patiently and stroked his chin thoughtfully. When Siegfried's outburst had ended in a confused whisper, Herr Hempel spoke kindly but honestly.

'Siegfried, you're a good chap, the kind of boy the Fatherland needs, a natural leader,' he told him. 'But it is as simple as this — and I say this without malice, believe me. If you are not with us, you are against us. There can only be one gang now. And we must all be part of it.'

His brave face pale and lined with sorrow, Siegfried turned to go.

'I know you'll join us,' Herr Hempel added. 'Only don't leave it too late. If I have my way, you'll be our Hitler Youth Leader. Remember that.'

At the Gang room table, Siegfried smiles again at the memory of those words — words that have echoed in his mind ever since. But then from above he hears the muffled tread of hurrying feet. I'll give them one last chance, he thinks, just one last chance. Even if Anna's father was almost certainly involved in the burning of the Village Hall, he can't very well blame her. Even if Dieter is, more often than not, little more than a millstone around his neck, slow in mind and body, Siegfried can't cast him aside.

Such are his misguided notions as he decides how he will test their worth — and his own worth in the eyes of the village. Anna appears, framed in the curved stone arch. Her dark hair is drenched with sweat, her arms filled with white roses and purple heather.

'Sorry I'm late, but I just couldn't resist these flowers.'

From behind Anna, Dieter jerks forward, the empty sleeve of his filthy coat swinging carelessly.

'S-s-sorry....'

'It's all right, Dieter,' Siegfried says despite his annoyance.

'I g-got lost again!'

The path through the wood from the village is a short and straightforward one. Not for the first time, Siegfried wonders how anyone can possibly lose their way there. His own four-year-old brother, Karl, has often toddled up to the Castle to call Siegfried for his dinner.

Finally, after Anna insists on arranging the flowers, the meeting is called to order. Greta reads the Secretary's Report in her usual assured way. There are no frivolous jokes, only a clear matter-of-fact detailing of the past week's activities. An excursion to the Ebsee Lake five miles away; the progress on the new tree-house they've started alongside the path, which is to be used as a look-out point; the plans for a twenty-mile hike to next month's County Fair at Tergensee Gardens.

'T-twenty!' Dieter exclaims, but is silenced by Siegfried's cutting glance.

'Anna,' Siegfried asks, 'could you give us the Treasurer's Report, please?'

Anna's olive-skinned face reddens as she searches the many pockets of her woollen cardigan.

'I seem to have left it at home. I'm sorry.'

Siegfried turns to Greta. He tries not to let her obvious suspicion remind him of their recent problems with money. Somehow the accounts, which are small anyway, never quite seem to add up these days. Anna's only answer to his enquiries, carefully put not to offend her, never come to anything more than an insincere simper. He decides to ignore the matter for now and press on with his plan.

'Maybe you'll have your report for the next meeting. Now, I have something important to put to you all.'

Anna's practised smile wavers and Dieter sighs at the prospect of yet again being stirred into action by the energetic Siegfried. Only Greta sits forward in pleasant expectation.

'You all know what happened to our new Village Hall,' he begins, choosing his words with the utmost care, 'and that what happened was wrong. The Lingen Gang has always fought against wrong, and if we're to survive as a gang we have to do the same this time.'

Dieter and Anna grow uneasy. As if to reassure them, Siegfried's tone becomes more mellow.

'Some people have jumped to conclusions about this crime,' he continues. 'But I'm.... we should be determined to catch the real culprits ...'

He looks above their heads so as not to catch their eyes or signal suspicion.

'... whoever they may be.'

'B-but if no one else c-c-could find them, how c-can we?'

'That was never a problem before,' Siegfried asserts. 'Who found the missing bicycles at Herr Dielen's? And who rescued my brother Karl when the whole village had given up hope for him?'

'The L-Lingen Gang!' Dieter blurts out with foolish pride; but then, pausing to think, he adds, 'B-but how.... where do we sta-start?'

All eyes turn to Siegfried.

'Herr Hempel is sure there's some clue to be found at the Village Hall but they haven't yet found it. Don't you see, this is what we've always been preparing for — the chance to solve a real mystery and bring real criminals to justice.'

To Siegfried's surprise Anna pipes up merrily.

'Yes, why not? I bet there's a big reward. Think of all the things we could buy.'

Has she no inkling that her father is the prime suspect? Or does she know and simply not care, the money more important to her than her father's safety? Is she, perhaps, so sure of her father's criminal abilities that she feels sure he has left no evidence? Putting these questions to the back of his mind for the present, he unfolds his plan.

At seven this evening there's to be a meeting in Herr Hempel's large house, which is at the other end of the village from the Hall. Siegfried's guess is that the Hall will be left unguarded for an hour, perhaps even longer. It will provide the perfect opportunity to explore those fire-cracked ruins.

The plan is quickly agreed to and arrangements are made to meet at two minutes to seven at the Hall. As they hurry home by the tree-lined path, Anna and Dieter soon fall behind and Greta whispers anxiously, 'If Anna's father is caught up in this and if — well, I don't mean to doubt her, but if she knows something about it, won't she tell him what we aim to do?'

'I've just been thinking the same thing,' Siegfried says, checking his watch. 'It's six o'clock, Greta. The Hall will be empty now. They'll all have gone home to eat.'

Siegfried clenches his jaw tightly, girding his strength for this, his first act of deception against the members of the Lingen Gang.

'We'll search the Hall. Now. Just you and me.'

At the outskirts of the village he looks across the whitewashed gables with their triangles of black-painted timber and across at the shingled rooftops. Red flags adorned with black swastikas hang from many windows, expressing the people's fervour for the changes brought about by our Fuhrer. Siegfried's heart is heavy. How can he refuse the call to arms of the Great One?

Greta senses his discomfort.

'Everything will work out for the best,' she says.

'I hope so,' he answers. 'And I hope with all my heart that I'm wrong not to trust Anna and Dieter. I really do.'

~

The village of Leiningen, built along the lower slope of Lingen Peak, has three descending streets. The upper one is Oberstrasse; the middle one, Mittelstrasse; and the lower, Unterstrasse. At the top end of Oberstrasse lie the remains of the Village Hall. Siegfried and Greta pass by the backs of the houses on Oberstrasse and enter the Hall from the rear.

As Siegfried had presumed, the Hall is unguarded. They set about their search quietly and methodically. Siegfried lifts broken beams and fallen blocks for Greta to rummage beneath.

In the beginning, time slips by slowly as if keeping pace with the deliberate care of their investigation. In a short time, however, Siegfried finds that he is looking at his watch more and more often. The impossibility of their mission begins to overwhelm him, and but for Greta's persistence he might easily give up the search as the Church clock clangs out the half-hour over the tranquil village.

'We'll find something,' she urges. 'We always do.'

Summoning up the last reserves of his strength, Siegfried lifts a huge slab of concrete and, his face streaming with sweat, casts it aside. Grey dust swirls about. Each particle is lit up by the criss-cross of sunbeams coming through the gaps in the damaged roof.

Suddenly their eyes are drawn to one narrow, precise wand of light. They follow its sword-like trail from the roof to the rubble below. There, sparkling like a diamond embedded in rock, is the object of their quest.

His heart pounding in his chest, Siegfried stoops low, takes hold of the prize and raises his hand into the light. Greta's breath comes quick and low.

'It's the lid from a petrol can,' Siegfried whispers.

He blows the dust from it and sees that it's quite new and undamaged by the fire it helped to unleash. He looks closer and, with a shudder, clenches it tightly in his fist. He presses his fist to his forehead and clamps his eyes shut to contain his pain and fury. Greta approaches and touches his hand. It opens like a flower.

On the underside of the lid two initials are etched roughly in the tinny metal. 'K.M.'

'Karl Matthias,' Greta gasps. 'Anna's father!'

A MORE WILLING WRITER

Flung from the nightmare of the new Leiningen, Siegfried lay on the floor of the Grey Room. His mind was his own again — at least until the next call of the typewriter bore him back to that mountain heaven that was now as hellish as the city outside Axel's attic room. He had drifted back to Leiningen knowing little or nothing of the new Germany and returned with the terrible knowledge that everything had changed. A new god reigned there, a god of prejudice and suspicion: Adolf Hitler.

How much more innocent the adventures of the past had been! The tale of the missing bicycles, not stolen but hidden away by the blacksmith. Herr Dielen's business had been struggling and his young family often went hungry. In the end, he blamed the sharp decrease in horses to be shod on the increase in the number of bicycles in the village, and took drastic action.

Every bicycle he could lay his hands on, he buried in the plot behind his forge. He wrapped each one carefully so they wouldn't rust. In time, he'd concluded, people would return to buying horses and relish the pleasure of the old ways so much that they'd ignore the bicycles he would unearth, one by one, and return to where he'd found them.

The Lingen Gang, naturally, were the ones who saw through this misguided scheme. In the story's conclusion they were able to convince him that the bicycle, like many new inventions, was not something to fear. The thing to do was accept them and, indeed, take some advantage from them. The book ended with the Grand Opening of Herr Dielen's bicycle repair shop which his son would work in. Like all the Lingen Gang stories, it had a good and timely moral to offer — that is, like all the stories until now.

If the transformation of Leiningen was great, the change in its people was even more drastic. Herr Hempel, the mild-mannered Stationmaster, spoke of a revenge that would be 'terrible'. The baker, Herr Stiefel, always so good-humoured, was reduced to bitter tears.

The Lingen Gang too had never been portrayed like this. All the talk of Secretary and Treasurer and reading reports left Siegfried bemused. One thing was clear to him. This 'more willing writer', whoever he was, had never read Axel's stories. If he had, he would have known that the Gang wasn't organised like some Local Council. There had never been all that formality that adults need to surround themselves with.

Anna, the dreamer and lover of nature, was now a sly and unconvincing liar. Dieter, for long the joker of the Lingen Gang, was no more than a stuttering simpleton. As for Greta, her thoughtful seriousness had taken on a dangerous edge of icy coldness.

Worst of all was the change in Siegfried himself. No longer trusting and true to the others, he was filled with unproven doubts about them. Strange obsessions had been thrust upon him, obsessions that sent waves of nausea through him — obsessions with Adolf Hitler, with the Fatherland, with the Hitler Youth.

He raised himself from the ashes of the Grey Room floor and went towards the vaporous table. As before, the others sat motionless. He resisted the temptation to tug at their outstretched arms.

If this was to be the last Lingen Gang story, then what was to become of them? Would each one disappear forever? Or would he and Greta be allowed to survive and act out a whole series of hateful escapades, while Anna and Dieter were consigned to an empty eternity? If this was so, he must stop it. But how? How, when he was more insignificant than the tiniest of insects in the real world outside?

Siegfried leaned back against the wall. He closed his eyes and suddenly felt something flapping against the side of his face. Some rough, dry clothy stuff like — like a grain sack. He looked around to get his bearings. Sure enough, the two curtained archways stood, as always, a little way off to each end. He turned and faced what should have been a blank wall, and stepped back in astonishment. A third archway!

This must be the passage to the new writer's house. Siegfried had no choice but to enter. He had to change this stranger's mind about continuing with that loathsome story.

A high, ornately-plastered ceiling crowned the large bed-chamber. At first glimpse, the furnishings and fabrics spoke of wealth and opulence. As Siegfried's eyes got used to the dim yellow light from the bedside lamp, however, he saw that the seeming splendour was somewhat faded. The long bobbled curtains were worn to a thread at the edges. The carpet beneath his feet was trodden in patches that exposed the timber floorboards beneath.

This writer, if once rich, had fallen on hard times or grown miserly. The image of a miser seemed to Siegfried to fit better. Who would carry out the dirty work of SS Haupsturmfuhrer Teufel but a man prepared to do anything for money?

Siegfried glided towards the vast four-poster bed. The big tapestried canopy overhead was just as moth-eaten as the long curtain. Beside the blackened crystal bedside lamp, the contents of a half-empty wine bottle cast a deep purple glow over a withered old face in a sunken pillow. Wisps of grey-white hair coursed out over the stained pillowcase. From the corner of the old man's mouth a track of dried-up red spittle led to his chin.

Drawing closer, Siegfried was assailed by the poisonous, vinegary smell of stale alcohol. The old man murmured fretfully in his dizzy sleep and his head rolled over and back on the pillow like a pock-marked stone that would never come to rest. Siegfried was sickened by the thought that the fate of the Lingen Gang lay in those wretched hands scrambling about like demented white spiders on the bedcover.

Close by the bed was a richly-carved writing desk. At its centre stood a typewriter flanked by a pile of crisp white pages. Siegfried peered at the top page.

'The Last of the Lingen Gang: Part 1,' it read. 'Siegfried Geistengel stands on the tumbledown parapet above the ruins of Leiningen Castle....'

Alongside the pages lay a bundle of envelopes all addressed to 'Herr Hans Gott'. On top of the desk was a photograph in a silver frame. There, a young couple smiled out from their wedding day but the woman's eyes betrayed a vague wistfulness.

In the bed, the old man was growing even more uneasy and Siegfried was sure he was about to wake. He knew he shouldn't feel afraid. Neither Axel nor the SS man had been able to see or hear him earlier.

No one, either in the Grey Room or in this real city of Berlin, could see him. Only in the dreamland of Leiningen was he visible. But the Siegfried the villagers saw was not the Siegfried he wanted to be. If he didn't act soon, he'd be plunged back into that place. Herr Gott's sleep was so disturbed that the return to Leiningen could happen at any moment.

'If I take these pages he's typed, then he'll have to start all over again — and I can keep taking them until he gives up.'

His chest swelled with relief and he laughed aloud to think it was so easy when, moments before, all had seemed irretrievably lost. He lowered his hands to pick up the loose pages.

They wouldn't be moved. He tried again but though he could grasp them, he couldn't lift them. They might as well have been fashioned from the heaviest metal in the universe, so immovable were they.

Herr Gott sprang forward in the bed and gaped, swaying, around the room.

'Who's there?' As Siegfried fled, the uppermost page on the writing desk flapped briefly and was still. The old man's glazed eyes narrowed and settled on the writing desk unhappily.

'This damned book,' he muttered, too brokenly for Siegfried to hear as he pressed back into the Grey Room, 'will be the end of me.'

He threw back the bedclothes and tottered shiveringly towards the typewriter.

'I can't go on,' he said. 'I must go on.'

Reaching back for the bottle on the bedside table, he raised the wine to his lips and swallowed long and hard until it was gone. He sat down at the desk, looked sadly at the silver-framed photograph and began to bang out the letters.

'P' — 'A' — 'R' — 'T'...

He slammed his finger on the number '2'.

The protesting cries of the boy in the Grey Room went unheard and soon fell silent. The irresistible call to Leiningen was answered once again by the Lingen Gang.

THE LAST
OF THE
LINGEN GANG

PART 2

Half a mile below the village and just beyond the Railway Station stands the Geistengel farm. Five generations of Geistengels have worked its thirty-five valley acres and one day it will be Siegfried's. He loves the sweat and toil of farming and loves the very soil of this fertile place. Today, however, he's distracted from his usual feeling of pride when the Unterlingen Farm comes into view. He has twenty-five minutes to eat and return to the Village Hall by seven for the search that will now be a mere pretence.

The family is already at table when he bursts into the kitchen with apologies tripping from his tongue. His father Heinrich, an honest forthright type, makes no effort to hide his displeasure. His voice rings deep and sonorous as the true music of Germany when he speaks above the busy chatter of Siegfried's three younger brothers and two older sisters, each one fairer than the next.

'We do not keep Mother waiting like this.'

'I'm sorry, Father,' Siegfried says and turns to his red-cheeked mother. 'I'm very sorry, Mother.'

Reassured by her open smile, he sits down and waits for his father to allow them to begin eating. Not one for making excuses, Siegfried wishes he could tell them what it was that delayed him. He says nothing, not wanting to plunge this happy German family into unpleasantness.

'Malzeit,' his father intones and they begin.

The boys, Heni, Max and Karl, eat ravenously. The girls, Frieda and Martha, remind them of their manners, as is their habit and duty. Siegfried eats in silence, trying to disguise his hurry. Heinrich, dreamily planning tomorrow's labours, appears not to notice. His wife is more sensitive to Siegfried's restiveness. No words need to pass between them.

The meal of garlic sausage, fried potatoes and baked beans is soon devoured. As they wait for the sweet, tangy promise of split tangerines, Heinrich stirs himself from his daydream and regards Siegfried. His solid features soften as he addresses his son, who is sneaking a look at his watch.

'Herr Hempel has been asking about you again, Siegfried. He thinks very highly of you, you know.'

The Railway Station and the Unterlingen Farm being so near each other, hardly a day passes but Herr Hempel and Heinrich meet. Their conversation always drifts towards the same subject: Siegfried's qualities of leadership. Heinrich is clearly anxious that his son take Herr Hempel's advice and join the Hitler Youth.

'I talked to Herr Hempel this morning,' Siegfried says.

Heinrich brightens on hearing this and his wife nods knowingly.

'Very good, then. I'll say no more on the subject. I'll leave it to you.'

Grateful for his father's trust, Siegfried feels at the same time a keen sense of guilt at his hurry to be away. He can't bring himself to stand up from the table, in spite of his watch's warning that it's now five minutes to seven.

'Hadn't you better go, then?' his mother suggests.

'Go?'

Heinrich's weather-sculpted face breaks into a grin.

'You've been acting like you're sitting on a beehive for the last twenty minutes,' he laughs. 'You'd better run before they start to sting!'

Siegfried springs to his feet and makes for the door.

'Another adventure?' his father wonders with a tolerant smile.

'Yes, but it's different this time. And Father?'

'Yes?'

Siegfried's arm shoots out straight as a stanchion of iron.

'Heil Hitler!'

Heinrich stands proudly at the head of the family table and answers the salute.

'Heil Hitler!'

At one minute before seven Siegfried reaches the shell of the Village Hall. Greta is there and, as he's expected, she's alone. The petrol can lid burns like a hot coal in his pocket as he scans the empty cobblestone streets for a glimpse of Anna or Dieter. The golden light of the low evening sun softens the stark white of the descending houses. It seems impossible that evil can lurk in this place. Impossible — until he turns to see the ravaged Hall. Impossible — until he hears in the distance Dieter's clumsily stammering whistle.

'The whole village will hear him coming,' Siegfried rages.

Dieter lurches around the corner into Oberstrasse. Siegfried places his finger to his lips to quieten Dieter. The gesture means nothing to the dim-witted boy and he calls out happily, 'I'm n-nearly early!'

The touch of Greta's saving hand on his arm calms Siegfried. Struggling up the steep incline, Dieter slows to a crawling pace. Pity fills Siegfried's heart; but, he thinks, pity is useless. He quickly sets aside the urge to go and help the boy. Dieter must learn to cope for himself, that much is clear.

For the first time, Siegfried realises that Dieter needs some kind of special help, some kind of training that will help him to live an independent life. Siegfried's own efforts have brought little success and Dieter is as dependent on him as ever. If only there was someone who knew what to do with a boy like this. A time might come when Siegfried was no longer around. What would Dieter do then?

'W-we'll never f-find anything in there,' Dieter complains, pointing at the Hall.

'Maybe you're right,' Siegfried says. He looks along Oberstrasse, feeling certain that Anna will not be coming.

Though she's spurned the second chance he's given her, he wants to let her have one more opportunity to redeem herself. There's only one thing for it. He will have to go to her house and talk to her. He can't tell her directly what he knows, but he'll hint at the truth and see if she's prepared to be honest with him. He watches Dieter kick despondently at a clod of singed timber and steels himself for the white lie he has to tell.

'Let's forget it,' he says. 'If the others haven't found any evidence, how can we? There's just the three of us.'

Dieter gurgles with relief.

'W-will we g-go and ask p-people if they've any sp-spare planks for the t-treehouse?'

'There's no point,' Greta explains. 'Everyone's at the meeting in Herr Hempel's.'

'N-not everyone.'

Dieter's answer, for all its seeming innocence, cuts Siegfried to the quick. 'Not everyone.' Siegfried remembers Herr Hempel's words: 'If you're not with us, you're against us.' He too should be at the meeting of the villagers, but there is work to be done. He can only hope that all those people will forgive him when they find out that he's trying to root out the devils in their midst.

'I'm going home,' he announces.

One furtive glance convinces Dieter that his usual pleas will be in vain. He begins to shuffle down Oberstrasse with shoulders hunched and face twisted to a sad clown's weepy grin.

'See you tomorrow, Dieter,' Siegfried calls.

'You're doing the right thing,' Greta tells him as Dieter passes from their sight.

'I hardly know what I'm doing any more. Or why.'

'Whatever you have in mind, I'm sure it'll be for the sake of the Fatherland, for the Fuhrer.'

'But I should be at the meeting. With my people.'

Greta's freckled face shines in the fading sunlight with a glowing ease.

'I'll go to Herr Hempel's,' she says. 'You go and do what you have to do.'

They leave the Village Hall, and as they reach the lower end of Oberstrasse Siegfried tells her where he is about to go. She gives him the reassurance he needs with her quiet nod of assent. Then she says, 'Siegfried, I've got my papers for the League of German Girls. I really want to join.'

'It's for the best,' he sighs. 'But wait a few days to sign them. We'll solve this mystery and the Lingen Gang can die with some pride.'

'Of course,' she agrees, and heads for Herr Hempel's.

Siegfried turns into Mittelstrasse and walks towards the last house on the pretty street. The house of Karl Matthias.

His first knock goes unanswered, and with each one that follows his mouth dries up a little more. The hushed conversation he heard from within, before he raised his hand to the star-shaped knocker, has stopped altogether. Siegfried senses that it's not merely a family gathering inside. When the door finally opens, Siegfried stumbles back in surprise. He hadn't heard the stealthy steps of the Jew approaching.

He sees one deep-set black eye below a bushy eyebrow. The full black beard moves with each syllable from the half-hidden mouth.

'Anna is not well,' Karl Matthias mutters. 'She's resting.'

'Couldn't I see her for just....'

'I'm afraid not. Maybe tomorrow,' Matthias says, and adds bitterly, 'Shouldn't you be at Hempel's — like everyone else?'

The door closes in Siegfried's face and all his unwelcome suspicions seem confirmed. Karl Matthias always greeted Anna's friends warmly. Was it ever a heartfelt warmth? Siegfried wonders, now that he's seen the real face of the Jew.

He steps back from the narrow footpath to the cobbled street and is about to turn away when he notices that the door of the small woodshed, built on to the gable of the Matthias house, is slightly ajar. On a sudden impulse he eases the door inwards and slips inside. In the half-darkness he sees, strewn about the untidy shed, the tools of Matthias's watch-making trade. There are also the many bits and pieces the villagers have given him in exchange for money loans.

Among the watches and mantel-clocks are cut-glass vases, framed embroideries and medals of honour from the 1914–1918 War. Each of these precious objects was of huge importance to the family who sold it for a pittance. Times have been hard and people have had no choice but to sell their family heirlooms. Surely now with the dawn of Adolf Hitler's Third Reich, Siegfried thinks, they will never again be reduced to swapping their German heritage for the price of a loaf of bread.

Without knowing exactly what he is searching for, he looks beneath rough workbenches and among dusty piles of junk. A steady stream of muted conversation comes through the thin wall between the woodshed and the house. Pressing his ear to the wall, he hears the voices of several men but can't distinguish who they are — except for Matthias, who is doing most of the talking.

As he listens his eyes settle on an old yellowed cow horn once used by some farmer to call his animals from the mountainside. He picks it up carefully from among the rusty metal boxes where it lies. He places the wider end of the warped funnel against the wall and puts his ear to the other end.

'... trains ...' The word blasts into his ear in a rush of stormy air that threatens to burst his eardrum.

Painful as it is, he has to hear more.

'... must get into the Railway Sta ... Hempel's out ...'

Karl Matthias's deep tones become more subdued until only a low mumbling can be heard. However, the few snatches Siegfried has grasped seem to point in one very clear direction. If the Village Hall was the conspirators' first target then the Railway Station is to be their next.

Siegfried sets the cow horn back in its resting place. Then he sees what was there before him all this time, though he was too intent on deciphering the voices from the house to notice. At the bottom of the carelessly-stacked metal boxes is a petrol can. The opening faces outwards. There is no lid.

He takes the initialled lid from his pocket. On his knees, he tries it for size on the can. It is a perfect fit. But the can is badly rusted and the lid is quite new. He has to be certain that the can has been recently used. He leans in closer and detects the sharp eye-watering odour of fresh petrol. The old lid had obviously become worn with time, or perhaps been lost, and was replaced.

Now he is fighting against time and against the mounting panic of his situation. If he is to take the can he will have to move each one of the boxes heaped above it and replace them so as not to alert Matthias. With each lull in the murmuring debate from the house his apprehension grows.

Only half the boxes have been set to one side when the scraping of chairs across a stone floor signals the end of the meeting in the house. He replaces as many of the cans as his trembling hands allow and goes to the door. There is nothing for it but to take a chance on stepping outside before the door of the house opens. His luck holds good. He gets to the other side of the street and slides into a steeply-descending and shaded alleyway. From here he can watch the conspirators emerge from Matthias's house.

The single window of Anna's bedroom stands high above between the steep inclines of the eaves. When Siegfried looks up he sees to his dismay that she's there, walking back and forth and not looking at all sick. The clasp on the front door below moves and Siegfried edges back into the shadows — and feels a hand on his back.

'C-can we go for the p-planks now, Siegfried?'

Half-incensed, half-relieved, Siegfried pushes Dieter lightly. Off balance, the one-armed boy slips backwards and totters on the verge of the steps that lead to Unterstrasse. Behind Siegfried, the door of the Matthias house opens and he catches a quick glimpse of the bearded Jew. The others, whoever they might be, are slower to come out and Siegfried is left with a cruel choice: leave Dieter to smash his weak-boned body on his downward flight, or go after him and miss his chance to identify the terrorists. He plunges down the steps to rescue Dieter, hoping he'll get back in time to see who Matthias's friends are.

When Siegfried eventually stops Dieter's fall, the cripple huddles against him. Crying at the sight of blood pouring from his knee, the boy whimpers dismally.

'You p-pushed me!'

'I didn't mean to,' Siegfried mutters, trying to pull free from the moist hand tugging at his shirt-front.

'Are you s-still my f-friend?'

'Of course I am.'

'W-will you always b-be? W-will you always help me?'

'Just wait here a second. There's something I have to do.'

He removes Dieter's hand gently from his shirt and climbs the steps quickly. Back on Mittelstrasse the door of the Matthias house is closed again. Dieter's fall, intended or not, has foiled Siegfried. He stares up at Anna's bedroom window but she's no longer to be seen. Has she been, he wonders, acting as a look-out — and not a very good one — for her father? Even yet, however, he can't quite believe she really approves of her father's treacherous intentions.

Of Karl Matthias's guilt he is absolutely certain. Knowing what he knows now, it might be better for him to go directly to Herr Hempel. His misdirected spirit of independence won't allow him to. The Lingen Gang might yet, he foolishly imagines, go out in a blaze of glory.

In this, he's not altogether wrong. Nor is he altogether right.

THE PRISONER

'Please speak to me!'

Siegfried's voice was small and feeble in the unrelieved gloom of the Grey Room. Living, or rather half-living, in two worlds equally beyond his control, he faltered on the very edge of madness. He weakly yelled his futile protests at his three companions.

'Don't ignore me. Don't leave me alone like this!'

He felt unclean, soiled by the things he was being forced to do in Leiningen. He rubbed his fingers roughly together, but the filth was in his mind and not in the hands that were less fragile now. He looked with revulsion, nevertheless, at the right hand that had just given its first Nazi salute. The memory of his imaginary family was even more disturbing.

What was it about his memory of them that filled him with such dread? It wasn't just the words put into their mouths by this Herr Gott. Something far more sinister bothered him. Their eyes. That was it. A terrible unseeing vacancy seemed to reside there — a deeper emptiness than in the eyes of his companions here in the Grey Room. It was suddenly clear to him that though he and Anna, Dieter and Greta might one day become fully human, those people never would.

His next thought was a devastating one. He, Siegfried Geistengel, was no more than the orphaned son of an imprisoned writer. Axel was all he had — Axel and the three silent ghosts before him, still as sleepers who'd lost the key to waking.

The boy with one arm sat stonily in his chair. His lips were white and slightly parted and there was a bloodless gash on his right knee. Siegfried tried in vain to figure out what his new creator had in mind for Dieter. All this talk of 'some kind of special help, some kind of training' went against the whole spirit of the Lingen Gang. They had always helped each other, all four of them. That had been the whole point of the Gang.

Looking at Anna, he remembered what Herr Gott had made of her father. Karl Matthias had always been like a jolly uncle to Siegfried. The beard, the dark brooding looks, the secrecy, were all new. Worse still was the inescapable fact that Karl Matthias shared the Geistengel family's blank gaze of unreality.

He turned to Greta. Her stark new coldness was tangible even here, beyond the world of Leiningen.

'He's made a monster of you too.'

At that moment, Siegfried was no longer certain, as he still was in Dieter's case and Anna's, that Greta would ever become real.

He looked from one to the next of the three archways around him: the Leiningen arch he'd just come through; the one leading to the decaying grandeur of Herr Gott's bedroom; and Axel's arch. He should have gone to Herr Gott and tried again to stop what was happening, but the courage to face the old man eluded him when he recalled his failure to lift even a single page from the writing desk. Entering Axel's room seemed more pointless still, and yet this was the choice he made. What he expected to find in that empty attic space he had no idea. To do nothing, to wait here for the typewriter to coax him back to Leiningen, would have been worse. He held back the curtain and went through.

Siegfried found himself not in the attic room but in a bare and windowless prison cell. The face of the prisoner sitting in the corner was hidden but was plainly Axel's. A strange new truth dawned on Siegfried. Wherever Axel was, in the attic room or this prison cell or anywhere in the world, he would always find him. The thought comforted Siegfried only very briefly. It mattered little that he could see his maker if Axel could neither see nor hear him.

From beyond the cell came the tortured cries of men and women in agony. Grown used by now to fear, Siegfried was faced with yet another disturbing emotion — hate. He had seen it in Teufel's steely eyes and in his dismissal of Jews and 'cripples'. He had seen it too in the Leiningen of this latest adventure. Now, hatred had wormed its way into his own heart. He hated Teufel and his black uniform. He hated the drink-sodden Herr Gott. He hated this whole hellish city of Berlin. Silently he cursed Axel for having created him and then left him to exist in this unbearable twilight between two worlds. He cursed until silence was no longer enough.

'Why have you forsaken me?'

Axel raised his head from between his knees and looked in Siegfried's direction. It seemed to Siegfried that their eyes met, but Axel saw nothing and merely lowered his bruised face again.

'Why can't you see me? Can't you try?'

This time Axel's response was more frightened. He peered fretfully about the cell, which was lit by a bare bulb high on the ceiling. He banged his forehead with the ball of his fist as if to unloose some mad thought from his mind. Barely able to contain his elation, Siegfried tested his new-found power once more.

'Axel? This is Siegfried. Siegfried Geistengel.'

Axel rose to his knees and the crazed leer on his lips astonished Siegfried. The coarse belly-laugh that followed drowned out Siegfried's repetition of his own name.

'I know this is some kind of trick, Teufel. You're trying to drive me out of my mind. But it's too late, Herr Haupsturmfuhrer, I'm already mad. I've been mad for years. Mad to have ever written a single word!'

'Axel, listen to me.'

'No. You're some kid Teufel hired to ...'

'I'm Siegfried. Your Siegfried. Please listen ...'

The heavy iron door shook in its frame, kicked once, twice by the guard outside.

'Shut up in there or you'll get another beating.'

Siegfried recognised the voice of Teufel's henchman, Wagner. Axel slid down along the paint-blistered wall of the cell.

'Please go away, whoever you are — whatever you are.'

Almost afraid to speak lest he should draw Wagner into the cell, Siegfried whispered, 'I *can't* go away, Axel.'

His words, filled with all the despair of his plight, silenced Axel's protests.

'Something's happening to me, Axel. I'm becoming real and I don't know what to do.'

Axel began to hum softly and press his hands against his ears. Siegfried felt another wave of hate flood through him. Hate was an easy habit to form. He charged at Axel, and the stormy vigour of his punches tossed his creator's hair about madly. Axel roared and lashed out his puny hands with as little effect as his ghostly attacker.

'Leave me alone! Leave me alone!'

Outside, the rough-hewn guard had had enough of listening to his prisoner's descent into madness. The door burst inwards and Siegfried tried in vain to stop the man from getting to Axel. His raging fists merely confused

Wagner and made him all the more determined to teach Axel a lesson. The assault was so merciless and Siegfried so weary from his efforts that he couldn't stay in the cell a moment longer.

In the Grey Room, Axel's cries seemed to come from some distant valley. Siegfried approached his three mute companions. He looked from one to the other. What right had he to wake them from their dreamless coma? Why should they have to suffer through the nightmare he himself was living?

The prison cell door banged shut and a huge quietness descended. In the old Lingen Gang stories, Siegfried often climbed to the highest, most inaccessible point in the ruins of Lingen Castle, far beyond where the others dared to go. There, undisturbed, he'd gather his thoughts on whatever mystery faced the gang. Without fail, he'd descend with some answer or some plan that would bring them closer to success. The same feeling of peace and mind-clearing calm took hold of him now. His thoughts took shape in a logical, orderly way and his sense of panic lessened.

Yes, he was to all intents and purposes alone in the Grey Room, but he no longer felt any anger towards his friends nor any wish to force them into wakefulness. And yes, once Herr Gott sat at his typewriter, as he soon must, Siegfried would be whisked back to Leiningen. But he would return from there and never truly be the Siegfried the old man wanted to make of him. It was true too that he'd failed to help Axel in his predicament, failed to stop the guard's bare-fisted attack. However, he was certain that Axel could hear him now and that he'd gained an invisible power like that of the wind. It wasn't much, but it was a beginning. He would grow even stronger. He was convinced of it.

A time would come when he was as strong in the world outside as he'd always been in Leiningen. He would have to be patient and use his present strange state to advantage.

That meant he must continue to visit Axel's prison cell, speak to him and, perhaps, share this new feeling of hope with him. As for Herr Gott, he mustn't give up trying to get through to him either. Even if Teufel found ten, a hundred, a thousand more willing writers, Siegfried would have to fight on. This book would never be completed while he had breath left in him.

Only when Anna, Greta and Dieter stood up slowly as one did Siegfried notice that the typewriter had started to sound. He didn't rage against its hold over him, but he repeated to himself, 'I'll be back. I *will* be back.'

Dieter and Greta were first to step beyond the Leiningen arch. Just as Anna reached it, Siegfried called to her, his thoughts drifting apart like a scattering crowd.

'I don't hate you, Anna.'

She turned to him. Her lips moved soundlessly. Her eyes seemed really to see him for a hazy, dreamlike instant and then she was gone. Siegfried followed, his mind already dead to the sudden surprise.

THE LAST
OF THE
LINGEN GANG

PART 3

Heinrich Geistengel and his son stroll up the narrow lane to the Unterlingen Farm. They are weary but in good spirits. For them, it's been a long, hard morning in the fields beneath the early sun. It's been even more difficult for Siegfried because he's slept so badly, troubled by his discoveries of the previous evening. The birds had already begun their chorus when he'd, at last, decided on his next course of action.

He would speak to Greta first, before the others appeared for their afternoon meeting. Greta would be told the full truth of what he'd heard at the Matthias house and of what he intended to do now. As for Anna and Dieter, they would simply be told that he was following a vague hunch.

The Gang would then split up in pairs. Anna would go with Greta to keep a watch on the backs of the houses on Oberstrasse. In fact, Greta would be keeping a watch on Anna and making sure she didn't find out where Siegfried and Dieter were actually going. Herr Stiefel's bakery, he would tell them.

Instead, he would head down to the Railway Station, bringing Dieter along so that he could have the one-armed boy in sight at all times. It's best to be safe, although he's convinced that Dieter is too slow-witted to be part of any conspiracy. In any case, he'd never figure out why they were hanging around the Railway Station.

Just as Siegfried and his father reach the farmhouse door and hear the welcome sizzle of frying from within, Herr Hempel calls cheerfully from the end of the lane. He strides towards them with a brown paper parcel under his arm. Heinrich is clearly pleased to see the village's first citizen. He's delighted, too, to see the parcel, which has aroused Siegfried's curiosity.

'Ah! You've brought it, then!' Heinrich declares. 'Come in and have a bite to eat with us. We'd be honoured.'

'Now, now,' Herr Hempel laughs, 'I'm the one who should feel honoured to sit with the true workers of the German soil.'

All through the meal Siegfried sits distracted by the unopened package in its resting place on the dresser behind his father. His sisters show no curiosity, as if they already know what it contains. The boys notice nothing but their food. Siegfried wishes his father and Herr Hempel would hurry with their eating and not talk quite so much between mouthfuls. His mother takes away his empty plate, which is just as well because he's about to start drumming out a protest on it with his fork.

At long last, however, Herr Hempel pushes his chair back from the table and slaps his broad stomach.

'Frau Geistengel,' he exclaims, 'can you come and teach my wife some of your culinary secrets?'

Siegfried's mother smiles shyly.

'With my flock there's only one secret, Herr Hempel,' she says. 'Fill the pot!'

'Heinrich,' Herr Hempel exhorts, 'why don't you try it on for us to see?'

Now even the younger boys are sitting up attentively. Heinrich takes the package into the sitting room, closing the dark-knotted timber door behind him. They wait excitedly for his return.

'I bet it's a new hat,' Max ventures. 'With a peacock's feather.'

'No, it's bigger than that,' Heni protests. 'A coat maybe, or...'

The girls swap amused glances. Siegfried feels like stamping on their feet under the table.

The sitting room door opens and Heinrich Geistengel stands tall, his chest expanded, in his new shirt. The earth-brown shirt of the SA, the Führer's stormtroopers — the Brownshirts.

'Meet our latest recruit,' Herr Hempel announces. 'A proud addition to our Local Section.'

Even as he claps and cheers with the rest, Siegfried feels a great weight spread over his shoulders. Now that his father has taken his rightful place in the Leiningen Brownshirts, how much longer can Siegfried delay his own entry into the Hitler Youth?

They drink a toast of pure spring water from the Geistengel well cut deep into the earth's heart by some long-ago ancestor. Amid all the high-spirited chatter Siegfried glances briefly at his watch and looks again in surprise. Half past two! The Gang meeting was set for quarter past. There is no chime on his watch nor even a clock in the kitchen to ring out but, somehow, a bell tolls in his mind — slowly, sonorously, like the village church bell tolls for a funeral.

He has never been late for a Gang meeting, not since the first day it was formed. He didn't intend to be late this time, but the fact that he is reminds him that there are more important things in life than the Lingen Gang. At this moment, he realises that the Lingen Gang is all but dead. All he can do now is try to make it an honourable death before he passes on to his new life as a Hitler Youth member.

'I'd better be getting back to the Station,' Herr Hempel says finally. 'We must keep the trains running on time!'

'And I've to meet ... meet someone,' Siegfried pipes up. 'I'll be home for the milking.'

'Well, we'll walk together to the gate then.'

The petrol can lid in Siegfried's pocket presses painfully against his thigh. A desperate urge to explain himself comes over him, but he can't find the words. Herr Hempel remains silent until they reach the end of the lane. When he speaks it's a relief for Siegfried to hear no ill-feeling in the man's voice, only concern.

'Have you thought about what I said yesterday?'

'Yes, I have, and I want to tell you ...'

'I've thought about it too,' Herr Hempel interrupts. 'And I'm worried that I may have sounded, well, a little too harsh.'

'Not at all.'

'I feel such a huge sense of urgency and of responsibility, Siegfried,' the Stationmaster sighs. 'Germany needs men like you if it's to take its place at the head of all the nations.'

Siegfried nods but still the words will not come. How to explain that he is ready to join the Hitler Youth, but can't bear to think that all his time with the Lingen Gang has been wasted? How to explain that if they can bring the terrorists to justice then he might feel he has achieved something with his gang? How to explain this innocent notion of his that some good can be got from the Jew and the cripple?

Even if he is mistaken, the dogged tenacity with which he clings to that notion proves that his is the truest of German hearts, loyal and trusting. But there are lessons he will soon learn about whom he should trust and to whom he should be loyal — loyal to the exclusion of all others.

Never before has Siegfried noticed the vile odour of mustiness and decay in the Castle basement. Dank green moss has smeared itself all over the walls. In a dark corner, a cluster of sickly pale mushrooms craves some light. He pushes aside the damp curtain with disgust and sees that he's the last to arrive.

'Where have *you* been?' Anna asks, cheekily delighting in his discomfort.

Just once, he thinks, I come late and she has the nerve to ask where I've been. However, he holds his tongue and walks confidently to his chair.

'Sorry about this, but we had an important visitor.'

'Th-that's all right,' Dieter stutters. 'I th-thought you mightn't c-come at all.'

At the sight of Dieter's tearful relief, Siegfried feels the same stomach-turning revulsion that filled him when he saw the slack fist of mushrooms. He goes quickly about his business. Greta makes no objection when he asks her to cut short her carefully prepared Secretary's Report. He scribbles a brief note explaining what he's about to tell the others and why. He hands it to her and says, matter-of-factly, 'Have a quick look at this and put it in your file. It's not important.'

Anna is so relieved not to have to read her falsified Treasurer's Report that she shows none of her usual inquisitiveness.

'We've very little to go on,' Siegfried begins. 'Nothing, in fact, except a hunch of mine that there are certain places in the village where we should keep our eyes open for any suspicious movements.'

Anna gives him one of her darkly searching looks but remains silent. Dieter is more enthusiastic.

'Your hunch was g-good enough to find the b-bicycles, S-Siggy!'

Siegfried is proud of his name. It's a name that reverberates with all the courage and power of the Germanic hero after whom he is called. He hates it when Dieter uses this ridiculous nickname.

'Dieter,' he says, forcing a smile, 'I won't call you Diddy if you don't call me Siggy.'

'B-but I don't mind what you c-call me,' Dieter grins. 'L-long as you d-don't call me too early in the m-morning!'

The joke, silly and infantile as it is, somehow relieves the tension in the evil-smelling Gang room and they all join in the laughter. Soon, the others are filing up the steps from the basement cellar. Siegfried stays behind and slips the petrol can lid from his pocket. He looks around for somewhere to hide it. Beneath the set of bookshelves on the far wall is his gold-painted trinket box, the one Dieter thinks is made of real gold.

It is filled with shells from his one and only visit to the seaside last year; toughened chestnuts which have won him many a conker fight; old coins and medals bearing the profiles of German heroes like Frederick the Great, Otto Von Bismarck and Field Marshal Von Hindenburg. He places the petrol can lid beneath these treasures, closes the box, replaces it and leaves.

Outside, at the entrance to the castle, Anna grasps Siegfried's arm and pulls him back behind the ivy-clad wall. Greta and Dieter have gone on. There is a terrible urgency lurking beneath her false sweetness.

'Why did you call yesterday evening?' she asks. 'If it's about the money I can explain everything.'

'Of course it wasn't the money,' Siegfried says, embarrassed but careful not to reveal anything. 'Just this crazy hunch of mine. I was going to tell you about it.'

'You were gong to tell *me* first,' she coos. 'How sweet of you.'

Siegfried blushes fiercely. The corners you paint yourself into, he thinks, when you lie. Even when the lies are necessary ones.

'What I meant to say was I was going to tell all of you,' he tries to explain, 'together. But you were sick so I decided to ...'

'I wasn't sick.'

If only she would tell him the truth now, then other truths might follow. It would be difficult for her but Siegfried feels sure she's very close to confessing all.

'You mustn't be afraid to tell me ... everything, Anna.'

'Everything?'

Anna's puzzlement is obvious as she slides away from him. His foolish optimism is fading with every step she takes.

'Father sent me to bed because I broke some stupid old vase. A silly pink thing, a family treasure he called it, the old goat. I'm glad I broke it, glad, I tell you.'

'Are you sure there's nothing else?'

She circles around him and begins to make a strange hissing sound. Siegfried isn't afraid but the feeling within the Castle walls is suddenly very unpleasant. A vicious look, like that of an escaping animal promising revenge, appears on Anna's face.

'You don't believe me, do you?' she spits. 'You're just like all the rest of them.'

When Siegfried reaches Greta's side, Anna and Dieter have moved on ahead.

'What did you say to Anna?'

'Nothing,' Siegfried tells her. 'But she lied to me about yesterday evening, I'm sure of it.'

They cross to the path leading to the village and soon catch sight of the pair up ahead. Anna has calmed down enough to co-operate with Siegfried's plan. As she and Greta walk down the lane behind Oberstrasse she can't resist a parting shot.

'It's too ridiculous. Watching and not knowing what we're supposed to be watching for.'

Every chance, Siegfried thinks, I gave you every chance.

'I d-don't know,' Dieter says merrily. 'I th-think it might be f-fun.'

'Idiot!' Anna mutters under her breath, and Siegfried is staggered by her rudeness. For all the clinging and snivelling he has put up with from Dieter, he has never dared say such a thing to him. At the bakery Dieter is still hurting in silence after Anna's mutterings. For a while they loiter about the street there without exchanging a word.

'You must take these things like a man, Dieter,' Siegfried says eventually.

'I d-don't ever want to b-be a m-man.'

Unwittingly, Dieter has put his finger on the real difference between them. Siegfried can't wait to become a man and do the things a man must do, for his family, for his Fatherland and Führer. Dieter, on the other hand, wants only to play in the Garden of Youth for the rest of his life. There is nothing to be gained from trying to convince him otherwise. Besides, it's time to move on to the Railway Station.

'I'm not sure if the bakery is such a good idea after all,' Siegfried says. 'Maybe we should try somewhere else.'

Dieter is too preoccupied with his slow, tortured thoughts to object and follows Siegfried listlessly out of the village. They sneak by the Unterlingen Farm but luckily no one is about the front of the house to see them passing. The last thing Siegfried needs now is to have one of his younger brothers on his heels.

The charming little station never fails to impress him. The neat greystone Stationmaster's office with its important-looking ticket desk; the well-watered window boxes of flowers; the tidy storehouse alongside the office; the small platform brushed as carefully and as often as many a kitchen floor ... All these things delight Siegfried, but there is something else that really takes his breath away. A single track sweeps out in wide and gentle curves in both directions and seems to him to lead to his manhood, to his future.

Few trains pass through here as this is just a small branch line; but, as Herr Hempel often reminds people, this doesn't make it any less important than the big city stations. One slight delay here might easily lead to chaos somewhere down the line. The smallest tasks, he wisely asserts, are the most vital of all. For example, he invariably adds — to Siegfried's dismay — if one man refuses to fight in a war then his country is all the weaker for it.

On this sunny afternoon the station is so peaceful it seems entirely deserted. There are no cars or carts at the entrance and Herr Hempel's office door is fastened with a heavy padlock. In spite of the light air of calm about the place Siegfried is more than a little disappointed. He sits on the wooden bench near the ticket desk, wondering if he's wasting his time. Surely, he thinks, these people can't be so stupid as to try anything in broad daylight? How can he have been so stupid himself as to think they might?

When Dieter whispers in his ear he almost jumps out of his skin, so far away has he drifted in his thoughts.

'Is that a b-bird or s-something?'

'What are you ...?' Siegfried mutters — and suddenly checks himself.

Now he can hear the gentle tapping noise and senses where

it's coming from. The telegraph machine in the ticket office. Moving closer to the half-opened window, he discerns the heavy, urgent breathing of ... But it can't be Herr Hempel. And if the only door of the office is so securely locked then how has anyone got in there?

'The window round the back,' Siegfried whispers in answer to his own question.

'The wh-what?' Dieter exclaims aloud, and inside the ticket office there's a sudden commotion.

Siegfried leaps towards the ticket desk but somehow Dieter gets in the way and they both go crashing to the ground.

'Wh-what did I d-do?' the cripple cries. 'Why d-did you hit me?'

'There's someone in the Station House,' Siegfried yells in exasperation. He springs up from the platform and peers inside the office.

The back window is ajar and receding footsteps echo around the spaces out behind. Siegfried sprints around to the entrance gate but, though he can see the road winding back to the village and the open fields behind the Station, there is no sign of the intruder.

So angry is he with Dieter that he can't think what to do next. He can almost believe the one-armed boy blocked him deliberately. Didn't the same thing happen up at the Matthias house? He tells himself to stop and think about the crisis in hand.

What could the intruder have been doing in there? Sending false signals down the line perhaps, or ... But it's useless to speculate. There is nothing for him to do but go inside the ticket office and hope that the terrorist has left some trace of his treachery.

Avoiding Dieter, who's still nursing a grazed elbow on the

platform, Siegfried goes around the back of the greystone building. He steps carefully over the window ledge. In here the air is stiflingly warm and filled with the heavy scent of ink and old paper ledgers. On a table below the ticket desk the telegraph machine stands silent now. Beside it, a notepad of yellowing pages lies. When he looks closer he sees that the top page is quite blank.

He sits on the leather seat at the table and, closing his eyes, he tries to imagine what it was the man had been doing. The palms of his hands rest lightly on the notepad. His mind is as blank as the page below his fingers. He feels so frustrated that he wants to grasp the heavily grained paper and roll it into a ball. Within seconds he's very glad he hasn't done so.

His fingers, working away independently of his confused brain, begin to find a track of indentations on the paper. Slowly, the message from his busy hands reaches his startled mind. His eyes shoot open. He looks at the uppermost sheet of paper. He picks up an old pencil stub and begins to shade lightly over the grainy surface.

When he's finished he stares at the faint but clear letters he's uncovered. The note is short and gives no explanation of its stark contents. He can only guess what precisely these terrorists have in mind. Another meeting? Or, worse, another burning? He reads through the words again.

'Tonight — stop — 1 a.m. — stop — Village School — end of message.'

WHERE HAVE YOU BEEN?

No sooner had Siegfried returned to the Grey Room than he was launching himself at the entrance to Herr Gott's den. The high-ceilinged chamber was empty, the far door open, and from beyond came the raised voices of a heated argument. The voices drew closer. One was tinged with fear, the other was contemptuous. The first was Herr Gott's, the second that of Hauptsturmführer Teufel.

The old writer stumbled into the room with such haste that it was clear he had been pushed. Fast at his heels came Teufel, snapping a menacing-looking riding crop against his shiny black boot. Herr Gott reached the bed and sat, cowering below the black-uniformed Hauptsturmführer.

'I was going to the shops, that's all. A man has to eat.'

'And drink?'

Herr Gott raised his hands in expectation of a blow, but Teufel had already begun to move around the room opening drawers, bookcases, trunks. Siegfried gazed in wonder as each hiding place revealed yet another store of empty wine bottles. Each bottle was flung into a gathering heap in the centre of the floor.

Much as he despised Teufel, Siegfried hoped the man in black would do what he himself so longed to do. Instead of beating Herr Gott, however, Teufel moved towards the bed and fished out some more bottles from beneath. Satisfied that his search was complete, he went and sat by the writing desk and began to leaf through the typed pages. Without raising his eyes from them he repeated his earlier question.

'And drink? You were going out for more drink, weren't you?'

'All these bottles, they've ... they've been here for years ... I ... I never got around to clearing them out ... These days I don't ... I don't drink at all.'

'I don't believe you, Gott.'

Teufel continued to read and fling each finished page back on the desk in an untidy pile.

'But it's true, I ...'

'Shut up.'

The Hauptsturmführer's attention seemed to be entirely on the script before him. He shook his head and tut-tutted every now and then. He showed little satisfaction in what he was reading, apart from one brief smile which soon froze over. Herr Gott grew paler with each discarded page. In the tense silence, Siegfried sank lower and lower in his corner.

When Teufel finally banged his fist on the writing desk, Herr Gott jumped to attention and stood on shaky legs, waiting for the worst.

'Come here.'

The old man padded across the glass-strewn floor and stopped just short of Teufel's reach.

'A little closer.'

In one agonisingly slow moment Herr Gott stepped forward, took a fierce punch in his stomach and staggered backwards to fall on the big bed. Siegfried took no pleasure from the old writer's suffering. He felt sick at having wanted this to happen.

'From now on, Gott, you'll not leave this room. Kroll will stand guard at your door and make arrangements for food to be delivered. But there'll be no wine, is that clear?'

Herr Gott, still doubled over on the bed, moaned.

'I'll take that as a "yes". Now, perhaps you'll be interested in my thoughts on your work so far?'

Another moan emerged from the pathetic heap of old bones.

'Ah, that's a "yes" also, I take it?'

Teufel took the bundle of typed pages in his black-gloved hand and waved it about as he spoke.

'Firstly, I don't mind saying that the story itself is, well, passable. Not wonderful, mind you, but it'll suffice.'

Herr Gott managed a nod of gratitude for this faint praise.

'However,' and the word had almost as bruising an effect as the vicious punch, 'however, there are problems. Problems I want sorted out immediately and not repeated. Yes?'

He didn't wait for a reply.

'The writing is too long-winded, the chapters are too long. You're not writing for adults, Gott, you're writing for mere children. Please keep that in mind.'

Sitting almost upright again, Herr Gott sighed in assent.

'What we want here is a book of no more than twenty thousand words. Eight, nine chapters at most. We don't want our children wasting every blessed minute reading, you know.'

'I see your point.'

'Good. And another thing. This ... this formality. For example, a wild undisciplined gang of youths doesn't have a Secretary and a Treasurer or organised meetings like this.'

Sitting in his corner, Siegfried was surprised to hear this echo of his own thoughts. It was an unpleasant shock to find that Teufel's mind and his own worked alike.

'And there are other more specific criticisms. For example, when Siegfried discovers that the Railway Station may be the next target of the conspirators, you say this ... let me see....'

Teufel shuffled through the pages and, finding the offending line, read it aloud.

"Knowing what he knows now, it *might* be better for him to go to Herr Hempel."

Herr Gott stared at Teufel quizzically. Siegfried too wondered what was wrong with those words.

'*Might*?' Teufel asked. '*Might*? You should have written something more definite. "Certainly would", for example. Do you understand?'

'Yes.'

'And then there's this confusing business in Part Three where Siegfried decides to tell only Greta of his plan to watch the Railway Station. Fine. But I read on expecting him to speak to Greta before the meeting. And what do I find? The meeting has begun and he writes some kind of note to explain the whole plan and passes it to her. This he does in the space of what ... a minute or so? Is this possible? Is this believable? I think not. Why do Siegfried and Greta not meet to discuss the plan before the meeting?'

Herr Gott's reply came in a warbling, high-pitched tone.

'It ... it slipped my mind that they were to meet. So, I had him write the note ... but I can change it if you ...'

'It slipped your mind because you were drunk, Gott.'

'No, I swear ...'

Siegfried flinched at the prospect of more violence. It didn't come.

'Well, we've sorted out that problem. Your mind will be clear now, not swimming in grape juice.'

Hauptsturmführer Teufel stood up and dusted off his peaked hat. He set the hat with its skull-and-crossbones insignia on his head and tucked the typed pages under his arm.

'One more small detail. You're not writing this thing quickly enough. Now that you've stopped drinking this shouldn't be too hard to correct.'

'I'll try to hurry it up, Herr Hauptsturmführer.'

'I'm afraid you'll have to do more than try or there'll be no payment. Now, I must return to my guest Herr Hoffen. I believe he may soon be changing his mind about taking the credit for this book of yours. Tomorrow night at eleven I shall call again and expect to see another chapter.'

When Teufel was safely out of sight, Siegfried got to his feet and moved towards the bed. His left foot touched a wine bottle which had rolled near him earlier. It spun away to crash into the pile of bottles at the centre of the room.

On the bed, Herr Gott sat up with a start, his eyes fixed in disbelief at the very spot Siegfried had reached. The old man followed every advancing footstep of Siegfried's. Or rather, he followed the impression made by Siegfried's invisible feet on the ancient carpet.

Herr Gott scurried back along the big double bed but the footsteps were no longer coming towards him. Siegfried had decided to test this new strength of his that had moved a thing as heavy as a wine bottle. At the writing desk he reached tremulously for the pile of blank pages and lifted the uppermost one.

Behind him he heard a gasp. Herr Gott watched in astonishment as the sheet rose as if by magic and remained suspended in mid-air trembling like an autumn leaf. Siegfried's hand was shaking. The sheet of paper was heavy but no longer impossibly so. He held it in both hands and with a long groan of exertion he crumpled it into a ball.

'Who is that? What ... what ...?'

Siegfried was so happy he didn't notice he'd been heard. He grabbed the next sheet and the next and crumpled those up too.

'My God!'

Siegfried spun around and stared at Herr Gott, who was clutching his chest and drooling from his purple-lipped mouth. In a frenzy of hate-filled vengeance Siegfried began to throw the balls of paper at his terrified target. He never missed, though the grey head weaved and bobbed frantically. With each hit he laughed louder. To Herr Gott it was the laughter of some devil and finally, overcome by the horror of it all, he heaved out a short gasp and tumbled from the bed to the floor beyond Siegfried's sight.

The sheet of paper in Siegfried's hand fell from his grasp and wafted slowly to the ground. He dashed around to the far side of the bed. Kneeling over the old man but afraid to touch him, he listened for the slightest trace of a breath. In his panic he heard none. The immensity of what he'd done sent him plunging back into the Grey Room. He staggered queasily into that dusty place — and suddenly froze.

'Where have you been?' a voice asked, a voice that in his confusion he didn't at first recognise.

He looked at his three companions. They sat at their usual places around the table. None of them showed any sign of having moved — except that around Anna's mouth a dry cloud of dust hovered like the smallest breath exhaled on a clear winter day. He approached the table and just as he got there Anna's grey lips parted.

'Where have you been?' she repeated.

Siegfried remembered that the words she'd spoken had come from the book, from the world of Leiningen. She was merely repeating them parrot-like. His heart sank.

Anna's eyelids fluttered once and came to rest. Her body began to shiver, delicately at first, but the shivering became more fierce until she was wracked with wild spasms. Her head and hands began to snap mechanically, faster and faster. The utter greyness of her skin was suffused with the tiniest hint of pink. The shaking stopped. Her eyes opened wide. Anna had come to life.

'Anna? Do you know who I am?'

The pounding of his heart was as overwhelming as in those first moments of his own coming to life.

'Siegfried! I don't understand. I'm afraid ... afraid of ... something....'

If Siegfried had been born to this new life through Axel Hoffen's fear, Anna had gained her life through Herr Gott's fear of an invisible tormentor.

There were no kisses in the Lingen Gang books, but Siegfried wanted to wrap his arms around Anna. But there was so much to tell her, so much to explain about this strange state of theirs.... The notion soon passed from his mind.

After some convincing Anna moved around the room with him. Gaining in confidence, she asked about the three doors and where they led. As gently as he could, Siegfried tried to explain the difficulties of this new life. He told her about Axel Hoffen and the name was immediately familiar to her. The names of Teufel and Herr Gott, though, meant nothing to her. He told her how this latest Lingen Gang book was intended to make examples of herself and Dieter.

He tried to explain the weakness of their bodies in the real world but was able, at least, to add that he was sure, that this wouldn't always be the case. He couldn't help saying, however, that the task of stopping this book seemed as yet an impossible one.

Once she had gotten used to the notion that she was no longer just an imaginary girl, her enthusiasm knew no bounds. Nothing he had to say could dampen her enthusiasm, and this surprised Siegfried. The fact was that in the Lingen Gang books, or at least in those of Axel Hoffen, the girls were always portrayed as softer and weaker than the boys and not up to the tougher challenges.

'It's wonderful. We can live our own lives.'

'It won't be easy, Anna.'

'Of course it won't — but nothing worthwhile ever comes easily.'

The phrase, echoing the oft-spoken words of Anna's father in the early Lingen Gang books, brought Siegfried back to the immediate problems they faced.

'There's something I haven't told you yet,' he said, turning towards the archway to Herr Gott's room. 'I think I may have killed Herr Gott. And I don't know what that means for us.'

'We'll have to go in there.'

'I can't. I can't face what I've done to him.'

'I'll go.'

Siegfried felt humiliated. The once-brave hero of the Lingen Gang was unable to muster the courage of his supposedly weaker companion. Only now was he able to consider the possibilities if the old writer really was dead. Either Teufel would find another 'willing writer' or he would abandon the project altogether. If he decided another Lingen Gang book wasn't worth the trouble, then what would become of them? Would he and Anna continue to grow into this new life? Would Greta and Dieter remain in the Grey Room for eternity?

He could find no answer to these questions. What he did know with certainty was that there would always be another writer who, by force or choice, might take up the writing of this fourth Lingen Gang story under Teufel's direction. If Siegfried had dealt with Herr Gott by accidentally killing him, how would he deal with the next writer — and the next? It could go on for months, perhaps years. If he ever did become fully human, was this what he wanted to spend his life doing? How could he ever enjoy life or be happy if this wearying battle with Teufel was all he had to look forward to?

Anna was beside him before he realised she'd returned.

'Siegfried?'

'I killed him, didn't I?'

'He's alive. He's lying on the bed crying over an old photograph. I couldn't see it but ...'

'Are you sure? Are you ...' Siegfried began, but when he looked at her she was staring at the archway leading to Axel Hoffen's prison cell. 'What's the matt —?'

A dull cacophony of screams and rough shouts came from beyond the curtained archway. Axel's screams; Teufel's shouts.

'We have to help him, Siegfried.'

'I've tried but it's no good. I ... we can't do anything for him.'

'We'll see about that.'

Anna rushed to the archway, swept back the curtain and called to Siegfried, 'Come on, don't just ...'

Her last words mingled distantly with the continuing racket in the cell.

'... stand there!'

Siegfried couldn't bear the thought of being alone, so he followed her.

Over by the heavy cell door, Teufel and the guard, Wagner, were taking turns at punching Axel. Behind them, Anna did what she could to restrain them, which, in truth, was very little. On the ground, a little way from the others, lay a large iron key ring with two outsized keys. Wagner had dropped them and hadn't yet noticed.

Siegfried remembered the wine bottle he had disturbed in Herr Gott's room.

Anna turned to him.

'About time! Aren't you going to do anything?'

His eyes were fixed on the keys and now Anna saw them too. She raced over to where they lay and tried to lift them. They wouldn't be budged. Siegfried walked slowly to her side and knelt as if in prayer. He wrapped the fingers of both hands around the metal ring and felt its coldness. A

deep groan emerged from him but was lost amid the uproar in the cell. He strained until the veins were etched on his neck and he clenched his teeth to stifle the animal yell that was welling up in him.

The metal ring rose from the ground and, as it did, it seemed to become lighter by degrees.

'You *will* put your name to this book, Hoffen,' Teufel was bellowing, 'or die.'

'Never!' Axel screamed, and winced in expectation of another blow.

'Wait,' Teufel said, stiffening suddenly.

The keys in Siegfried's hands tinkled and he was certain the Hauptsturmführer had sensed his presence. Very carefully he laid the metal ring on the floor, hoping that Teufel wouldn't turn around too quickly. But the man in black stood quite still and his attention never left Axel.

Siegfried looked at Anna and she pointed at the half-open cell door. He could see the bank of steps outside.

'We could go out there and see if there's a way to get Axel out of here,' she whispered. 'You're strong enough to lift the key. If you can lift it you can turn it in the lock, can't you?'

Before Siegfried could protest, Teufel was speaking again.

'You are a very foolish young man,' he said. For a moment, Siegfried imagined that Teufel was addressing him and not Axel. 'Very foolish. You seem to have no regard for your own life. We shall see if you have any regard for the lives of others.'

Siegfried reached the steps beyond the cell door quickly and, with the Hauptsturmführer's voice fading behind him, he climbed until he was faced with a timber door at the top. Through its glass panel he saw that it was unguarded. He tried the handle, certain that he wouldn't be able to open it. To his surprise it squeaked open and he went on, through door after door, hearing voices but seeing no one.

He came to a heavier double door, at the bottom of which was a long sliver of light. Guessing that this led to the street outside, he tried to figure out how it opened. There was no handle, just a long bar that refused to move though the door rattled on its hinges from his efforts.

Suddenly he heard someone approaching. There was no place to hide. He turned and was faced by a bespectacled man in a black boiler suit. There was no need to hide. This man saw no trace of him, any more than Teufel or Axel or Wagner had.

Siegfried moved aside as the man came closer and banged his fist upward against the long bar. The door came ajar and a flood of noise and light came through. Siegfried turned away so as not to be blinded and saw, on the ground below him, the faint but visible outline of his own shadow. He darted towards the dark corner by the door and pressed himself into it. The man looked up and down the street outside, shrugged, closed the door and went away scratching his head.

It seemed to take forever for Siegfried to find his way back. The long dimly-lit corridors were busier now, and he was forced to duck into doorways to avoid having his shadow seen as black-uniformed SS men passed by him. He tried not to panic as the minutes passed, but the terrible thought came to him that the cell door might be locked by now.

He travelled down one set of steps after another but the harsh voice of Teufel was nowhere to be heard. The building was a nightmarish maze — so many corridors that looked exactly alike, so many unnumbered doors.

Then he heard Axel's scream and the awful echo of it hung in the air long enough for Siegfried to find the right stairway. The door remained unlocked, but when he got inside Teufel had left and there was no sign of Anna.

The guard, his bald head bristling with sweat, hovered menacingly as Axel signed a sheet of typed paper. He had given in. His hand shook and guided the pen so uncertainly that it seemed as though he'd forgotten how to spell his own name or had even forgotten the very name itself.

'Don't think the beatings have stopped,' Wagner sneered, slipping his truncheon back into his belt.

When Siegfried saw the truncheon he knew how they would rescue Axel.

'Thank heavens, you're safe,' Anna said as he re-entered the Grey Room. 'They've persuaded him, Siegfried.'

'I know.'

'They told him they'd kill Herr Gott if he didn't agree. Teufel said his bosses are getting impatient, that the book must be finished soon or not at all.'

'But they'll find another writer if they have to.'

'No, Siegfried, I heard Teufel say there'd be no more time wasted on the book.'

So if Gott didn't finish the book that would be an end to it. Unfortunately, Siegfried had failed to get through to the old man yet. However, there was something they could do to upset Teufel's plans. If they could help Axel to escape, then this tour of schools and Hitler Youth meetings would have to be abandoned. That might just be enough to decide Teufel against the whole business. They could only hope that Greta and Dieter would have woken from their stupor by then.

'I think we can get Axel out of that hell-hole, Anna.'

'But how?'

'The guard's truncheon ...'

The typewriter in Herr Gott's room silenced Siegfried.

'We'll be back, Anna,' he thought. 'We'll ... be ... back!'

THE LAST
OF THE
LINGEN GANG

PART 4

Siegfried walks quickly up the path to the village, with Dieter stumbling along in a half-trot some yards behind him.

'D-did you f-find something? You d-did, d-didn't you? Why d-don't you t-tell me?'

Siegfried's answers are short and to the point. 'No.' 'No.' 'Because there's nothing to tell.' The time for niceties is over. When he comes to the spot where Greta and Anna are supposed to be on the look-out, Siegfried looks around impatiently to see where they've got to.

'Greta!' he calls angrily. 'Anna!'

He hears someone sobbing close by and steps forward to peer behind a high laurel hedge. There, Greta sits on a sloping bank of grass holding her hands to her face. Between the graceful but strong fingers of her left hand a single trickle of blood emerges.

'Who did this to you? Have they hurt Anna too?'

Greta shakes her head but doesn't look up — she's too

ashamed to face him with the tears still in her eyes. He kneels beside her. From behind he hears Dieter gasp and scuttle away at the sight of Greta's blood. Siegfried takes her hands away from her face. On her left cheek, four parallel scratches ooze red droplets.

'Who did this?'

'Anna.'

She speaks in an amazed voice as if she can't quite believe what she's saying.

'But why?'

'I told her I was joining the German League of Girls,' she says. 'I tried to make her understand but she wouldn't listen. I'm sorry, Siegfried, I shouldn't have but I just wanted to be honest with her. Was I wrong?'

'Of course not. But honesty means nothing to these creatures.'

As he looks down over the high roofs of Leiningen he finally accepts that the Lingen Gang has reached its end. No last triumph awaits its four ill-matched members. The right thing to do now is to go to Herr Hempel with his evidence of Matthias's guilt and this ominous message from the Railway Station. But, once again, wrong-headed pride gets in the way of good sense.

Surely, Siegfried thinks, he and Greta can salvage something from the wreckage of the Gang. If they can identify, once and for all, the real terrorists, and in the process stop them from attacking the school, then they will have achieved something. Selfishly he thinks that this will ensure his place as leader of the local Hitler Youth, which he's now decided he'll join tomorrow.

The Leiningen Schoolhouse lies just beyond the ravaged Village Hall at the upper end of the village. At twelve midnight,

Siegfried announces, he and Greta will take up position. Greta will hide in the burnt-out ruins of the Hall. Siegfried will be inside the schoolhouse with an oil lamp and a box of matches. They'll communicate with a system of owl-like signals they perfected in the bicycle adventure, and he'll be ready when Matthias and his friends arrive. Should they need to escape the clutches of Matthias, they'll go through the open fields above the village and meet at the Gang hut in the old castle.

By now, Greta is no longer listening to Siegfried but staring over his shoulder. Siegfried turns to find Dieter grinning sheepishly at him.

'And what will I d-do?'

'I thought you'd gone home.'

'It's a b-brilliant idea, Siggy ... Siegfried. How d-do you think of these th-things?'

It's five o'clock in the evening. Seven hours to midnight and Siegfried knows he can't let Dieter out of his sight. He can't trust him to keep the plan secret, whether or not he's involved in the Matthias conspiracy. But how is he to watch the one-armed boy for seven hours? It's almost suppertime and there are the evening chores to do.

'Dieter,' he says brightly, the problem solved, 'how would you like to have supper with us and stay the night? That way we can leave together before midnight. What do you say?'

Tears of gratitude well up in the cripple's eyes. An only son for whom his parents care little, he longs to be part of a big family, the kind of family that will make Germany great — though that isn't Dieter's concern. Like a little puppy, all he wants is the warmth of companionship, and the Geistengels seem to him to have more than their fair share of that.

'W-we'll be like b-brothers, Siegfried, w-won't we?'

The final arrangements agreed, Greta leaves for home and

Siegfried and Dieter walk out to the Unterlingen Farm. Dieter insists on knowing what part he'll play in the events to come.

'You can hold the box of matches when we're sneaking out to the school,' Siegfried tells him. 'It may not seem an important job but without the matches I can't light the lamp to see who these people are.'

'And when you and G-Greta are in your p-places where will I b-be?'

As far away as possible, Siegfried thinks. But no. Dieter has to be where either he or Greta can see him.

'You'll be hiding in the Village Hall with Greta.'

'I c-can't wait,' Dieter yelps, and gives a little skip that almost sends him tumbling.

The Geistengels welcome Dieter with open arms. Or rather, they can't find it in their hearts not to feed and give one night of decent shelter to the ragged and ill-shod boy. Before he brings Dieter out to help with the chores, his father takes Siegfried aside.

'We don't mind having the lad around from time to time,' he tells his son. 'But it pains me to see him so neglected by that stepmother of his and that drunken father. There's a place for boys like Dieter. A special school where he'd get proper care. I think maybe we should try to get him in there. I'm sure Herr Hempel would help.'

'But he'd have no friends there,' Siegfried protests.

'He'll make new friends,' Heinrich says. 'People like himself. You've done all you can for Dieter. No one could have done more. Believe me, this is for his own good.'

Siegfried realises that his father is right.

'There's a time when pity is no longer enough, Siegfried. We

must help him to help himself. That can never happen while
he lives in that ... that pigsty.'

Siegfried nods, ashamed of the softness in his heart that
won't quite go away.

'Good lad. I'll speak to Herr Hempel, then.'

The evening passes slowly. Chores that normally take two
hours at most are delayed time and again by the one-armed
boy's clumsiness. As the minutes drag on, Siegfried becomes
more and more convinced of his father's wisdom. A cruel
wisdom perhaps — but isn't all wisdom cruel, shattering as it
does our illusions?

When Siegfried asks his mother if he and Dieter can sleep
in the hayloft of the barn, she agrees so easily that he is
consumed with guilt. It bothers him that he'll soon be sneaking
out without permission but, as he sees it, he has no other
choice. He hopes she doesn't notice the rush of blood to his
cheeks as he gathers some blankets and crosses the neat
farmyard with Dieter.

They climb the sturdy ladder Heinrich built with his strong
hands and settle themselves. It's just past ten o'clock. Two
more hours to wait. It doesn't take long for Dieter's excited
babbling to subside. Field mice set the dry straw crackling
with their scurrying about.

'I'm af-afraid.'

'Don't be silly, they won't eat you.'

'B-but they might n-nibble at me!'

'Try to sleep, Dieter. You'll need to be on your toes come
midnight.'

But Dieter isn't ready for sleep just yet.

'The other d-day I thought of a b-brilliant idea for the
t-treehouse.'

Siegfried has forgotten completely about the treehouse.

They've done no more with it since setting the planks for the floor. It will never be finished now.

'I thought we c-could paint it,' Dieter continues enthusiastically. 'P-paint it *red*!"

'Eh, it wouldn't exactly be very secret if it was painted red,' Siegfried explains patiently.

'B-but I have the p-paint.'

'Did you steal it?'

Dieter looks away.

'Did you steal it, Dieter?'

'N-not exactly,' Dieter mutters.

'Where's the paint now?'

'Up in the t-treehouse. It's a real n-nice red.'

'Leave it back where you got it, all right?' Siegfried warns him. 'It's wrong to steal. Now get some sleep.'

'I c-can't sleep,' Dieter says disappointedly. But in a very short time he's snoring blissfully in the rough bed that's more comfortable than anything he's ever slept on before.

Only when the church bell rings the quarter hour before midnight does Siegfried realise that he too had drifted off. Knowing Greta as he does, he guesses that she's already making her way to the Village Hall. He shakes Dieter's shoulder.

'Time to go,' he whispers.

Bathed in silver moonlight, the village seems to Siegfried more perfect than any object fashioned from the most precious of metals. He and Dieter hurry along its narrow streets. Siegfried carries the oil lamp, Dieter carries the box of matches. Just as he thought, Greta is indeed waiting for them. They go through the plan once more, ensuring that every step is clear to all of them. Dieter, however, is as confused as ever. Finally, after yet another attempt to explain the details, Siegfried tells him more abruptly than he wishes to, 'Look, all you have to do is run back to the Castle when Greta tells you. Follow her, all right? And don't come near the schoolhouse, whatever happens. Do you understand?'

'B-but what if they c-catch you?'

'Just go with Greta. I can look after myself.'

Soon, Siegfried is climbing through a window at the side of the school and taking up position beneath a desk in the classroom, just inside the front door. In a moment of panic he remembers the matches. He's forgotten to get them from Dieter, and it's too late to go back outside. Did the one-armed boy deliberately neglect to remind him of the matches? Or will Dieter try to follow him into the schoolhouse with the things?

The muted whispers he hears seem, at first, to confirm his worst fears. Dieter? No. Something falls — something heavy with a dull metal ring to it. A petrol can?

Someone swears and the tone is unmistakably adult. A shadow, darker than the darkness outside, flits by the window and returns. The shadow of a bearded man.

Suddenly, all hell breaks loose. Glass explodes inwards. Siegfried pounces up and yells at the top of his voice, no words, just a scream. Outside, footsteps clamour in confusion as he sprints across the floor, his boots crunching through the splintered glass. He raises the window, not caring if his hands are cut to pieces. Luckily for him they aren't. He tumbles out into the night and on all fours he glances up at the high field behind the schoolhouse, where two men scramble away like rats from a sinking ship. Racing around to the front of the building, he looks up and down the street — and sees not a soul.

He stands there with his hands hanging uselessly at his sides.

He feels stupid; if he'd just waited a moment longer he might have caught a glimpse of the face by the window.

Then he remembers the oil lamp and goes back inside the schoolhouse to collect it. Among the glass shards on the floor he finds no clues. All he has to prove Matthias was here is the shadow of a beard, and that's not enough. There's no escaping the fact that he's bungled the whole episode. Only the combined effort of all the good people of the village can conquer evil and, at long last, Siegfried has learned that lesson.

The path to the Castle has never seemed so steep. His strength is sapped as surely as his pride. When he sees the ivy-clad ruins framed above him in the night sky he feels a terrible loneliness. But he knows that soon, tomorrow in fact, that loneliness will end. He'll take his place among the boys of the Hitler Youth and it doesn't matter to him any more whether or not he becomes their leader.

Ravens flutter noisily in the dense growth of ivy. Siegfried descends the damp steps to the dungeon below. He's ready to tell them that it's all over for the Lingen Gang. Greta will be relieved. And Dieter? Well, he'll have to be made to understand that it's for the best.

Siegfried pulls across the wet curtain.

'Who is it?' Greta whispers fearfully.

'It's me. Siegfried.'

Below Greta's blonde hair her face is ashen.

'They took Dieter,' she cries. 'We ran straight into them up in the fields.'

'Did you recognise them?'

'It was too dark and everything happened so quickly ... I'm sorry.'

'Don't blame yourself,' Siegfried tells her.

Though he fears for Dieter's safety, he also feels a keen sense of relief. If the terrorists have taken him prisoner then he can't be one of them. But what to do now? Go in search of Dieter, perhaps to Matthias's house? Wait here and hope that the one-armed boy will be released and find his way back to the Castle? Or go directly to Herr Hempel and tell him everything that has happened?

He makes up his mind to go to the Stationmaster in spite of the late hour. Then he hears a familiar shambling tread on the steps outside. Dieter bursts into the Gang room. His right eye is blackened and bruised, a red droplet hangs from his lower lip.

'S-Siggy, they b-beat me up,' he gasps. 'They said if we d-don't b-back off they'll k-kill us!'

'Who did this, Dieter?' Siegfried asks. 'You must have seen their faces or recognised their voices.'

'I d-don't know. Honest, I d-don't. I was s-so scared and they had th-things over their heads and ...'

They leave the Gang room and the Castle. Siegfried doesn't look back. All of that is in the past now; the Lingen Gang, those innocent days. When they reach Greta's house he finds himself shaking her hand, and it feels like the end of his childhood has come.

Back at the farm he settles Dieter in the hayloft and tells him he'll be back soon, not to worry. Dieter is strangely quiet, not insisting — as he normally might — on going too. He doesn't even ask where Siegfried is off to. There's no time to dwell on this curious fact, because Siegfried is already putting together in his mind the story he's about to tell Herr Hempel.

On his way he'll collect the petrol can lid from the trinket box in the Gang room. He hopes it'll be enough to convince Herr Hempel that Matthias is indeed the main culprit — and enough to prove his own worthiness to join the Hitler Youth.

A SINGLE SPARK

Axel Hoffen lay stretched on the cell floor. He'd fallen asleep there, too tired and defeated to care about the discomfort. At his side, Siegfried began to whisper in his creator's ear.

'I'm here, I'm here. Siegfried is here.'

Very reluctantly, Axel emerged from the dark chasm of his dreamless sleep. His eyelids flickered but didn't open. Siegfried knew he was awake and listening. The curious thing was that there was no incredulous outburst — only a look of resignation on the swollen face.

'Let me be. Just go away and let me die.'

'Never! I've come to release you. I think there's a way.'

Axel's eyes opened with a start and he seemed to stare directly at Siegfried. A terrible thought came to Siegfried. If Axel could see him, then the guard might see him too. That would surely be the end of his plan.

But there had been no sign of recognition on Axel's part and he had already looked away, though his look wasn't a distracted one. He gazed at a point on the floor beside him. Siegfried followed his gaze. There, foreshortened because they both knelt directly below the bare bulb, were two quite distinct shadows. Siegfried's own shadow was no longer the vague, insubstantial thing it had been out in the prison corridors earlier.

'Now do you believe me, Axel?'

'I think I always have. What about the others? Where are they?'

'Anna is here too.'

Axel peered about the cell and turned again to where he guessed Siegfried must be.

'She has no shadow, not yet.' Siegfried motioned to Anna and she drew nearer.

'Axel? This is Anna. Can you hear me?'

'Anna, you sound just as I'd imagined.'

'We're going to set you free.'

The determination in Anna's voice almost convinced Axel. Almost.

'No one leaves this place — except in a coffin.'

'We can do it,' Anna insisted. 'Siegfried has it all worked out, don't you, Siegfried?'

But Siegfried hadn't heard her. A bold new idea had occurred to him and he was thinking it through. Axel was disturbed by the silence that seemed to suggest Siegfried wasn't entirely convinced either.

'Siegfried?' Anna was getting impatient.

As Axel listened in growing wonder to his two creations, his sense of hope, shattered by Teufel's onslaughts, was returning to him. He remembered the simple joys of walking unhindered along the streets of Berlin, of sitting in a café, of talking with friends and acquaintances — all the joys he had, far too often, denied himself when he'd been free.

Soon he'd be free once more, and even if he was forced to live far from the country of his birth he'd never deny himself these things again. There was even the hope that one day he might return to Germany when this madness of Nazism passed, as it surely must.

'Siegfried?' Anna repeated. 'Why are you ignoring me?'

Siegfried smiled at her. He looked like a small child

emerging from a sweet-shop with pockets full of his favourite sweets.

'Well? Are you going to tell me what the big grin is for?'

'I have it! I know how we can stop this book once and for all ... at least, I think it might work ... I ...'

'You've already told me that. We get Axel away from here so he can't go promoting this horrible book, right?'

Axel was smiling too as he imagined the impatience on Anna's pretty face.

'No, there's more. What if Axel were to write the next chapter and make Hempel the villain instead of your father? Then we could switch Axel's chapter with Gott's and when Teufel sees it he'll go crazy. He'll think Gott is drinking again and call the whole thing off.'

It was as if they'd forgotten Axel was in the cell. Axel was greatly amused by the thought that two invisible people were speaking as though the only visible and fully real person there didn't exist. He felt his pain dissolve to be replaced by an extraordinary feeling of excitement. In a mad world, Siegfried's idea seemed to him perfectly sane.

'But Axel can't do that, Siegfried. He'll be too busy trying to get out of Germany. The smallest delay might cost him his life.'

'Maybe you're right. And besides, is there any real point in trying to stop this book? I mean, there'll be hundreds of other books written anyway, won't there? What difference will one less book make?'

There was no immediate answer from Anna but Axel, his senses fully alive, felt she was thinking hard about what Siegfried was saying.

'I don't mean we should give up, but there's only so much we can do, Anna. Free Axel, free ourselves, and hope Dieter and Greta wake before it's too late. As for the book — well, like I said, does it really matter if it's written?'

'And when the river's high ...' Anna began, and then

faltered. She clenched her fists in frustration, trying to remember, and tried again. This time the words came without a pause.

'"*And when the river's high*
  One single drop of water is enough
  To make a flood.
 And when the leaves are dry
  One single careless spark's enough
  To set alight the wood."'

Siegfried looked at her in amazement. If this poem had been in one of the Lingen Gang books he would have remembered it. But there was no poetry in those books.

'Where did you learn that?'

Anna had surprised herself as much as she surprised Siegfried. She had no idea where the words had come from.

'Oh, I don't know. But can't you see what it means? One book can make a difference no matter how many there are. And stopping one book can make a difference too.'

'I understand. I'd just like to know where that poem came from if it wasn't in the Gang books.'

'I wrote it,' Axel said. 'It was one of my *Night Songs*. One of the reasons I ended up in here.'

There was no despair in his voice. He felt strong again — stronger than he'd ever been in his life.

'I'll do it,' Axel said.

'Do what?' Siegfried was losing track of their conversation.

'Get me out of here and I'll write that chapter.'

'It's too dangerous.'

'Freedom always has a price, Anna. I'm sure you know that by now.'

Siegfried's last protest was half-hearted. 'But I haven't thought it through, Axel. Where will you get the typewriter and pages, and how....?'

'Let me worry about that.'

Siegfried and Anna exchanged glances and she nodded her approval.

'I hope my plan works.'

'It'll work,' Axel told the still air from which Siegfried's voice emerged.

Outside the cell door, Wagner's bulldog features were etched with a growing annoyance at the mutterings coming from within. Haupsturmfuhrer Teufel had warned him to hold off on the beatings for a while. He feared that the guard might do some permanent damage to Axel. That wouldn't look good on the tour of schools and Hitler Youth camps he'd planned for the writer. But Wagner could take no more when he heard the loud wailing which Axel Hoffen had now started up.

In his anger he had trouble finding the right key, which made his desire for revenge all the greater. Eventually he got the door open and swept inside, his truncheon swinging loosely by his side. With his big fists raised, he made for the prisoner. He felt something tug at his belt. The last things he remembered later were the crack on his skull and the prisoner's smile as the blood-red darkness fell.

The corridors were eerily quiet. Axel had no idea of the hour. In his basement cell, the light always left on, he'd lost track altogether of time. As they ascended the many sets of steps there wasn't a window in sight. Siegfried led the way, calling him softly on from one corridor to the next, each door opening by a magic Axel could now understand. With each door the thrill of escape and the fear of capture increased.

Siegfried advanced along what he knew was the last corridor before that barred door leading to the street.

Suddenly a door beside him swung open, and he was standing face to face with Teufel. The Haupsturmfuhrer paused — and turned back to someone in the room behind him. Siegfried grabbed the handle and pulled the door shut. With all his strength he resisted Teufel's efforts to prise it open. Axel ran down the corridor and pushed the bar upwards, as Siegfried had told him to, on the final door.

The cool night air brushed across his battered face as if it had already begun to work its healing power. The street was empty. Axel closed the door quietly and disappeared into the back streets of Berlin.

'What the hell is wrong with this door?' Teufel was demanding of an underling on the other side of the door from Siegfried.

At last, Teufel released his grip and Siegfried raced away to the door at the end of the corridor where Anna waited. Soon they were in the cell again, passing by the still-unconscious Wagner and on into the Grey Room. They listened for the dreaded sound of Axel being returned to his cell. At the table Greta and Dieter sat upright as before, their grey bodies quite still.

A tremendous tiredness soon overcame Siegfried and Anna. The long silence, at first so forbidding, became in time reassuring. They slept. Though their dreams were different, the place was the same: Leiningen.

Anna was walking in the fields above Lingen Castle with Greta. They picked flowers: edelweiss, white roses, snowdrops. Even as she gathered them Anna felt the oddness of all these flowers being in bloom in the same season. She wondered too why all the flowers were white ones. As they walked she tried to explain the strange new life that had blossomed in her, in all its wonder and terror. But Greta couldn't understand a word of what she said; she asked Anna to stop because it was frightening her.

Siegfried's dream too was odd. He found himself sitting at the big rough table in the Unterlingen farmhouse. Haupsturmfuhrer Teufel and Wagner sat before him, as grey and motionless as he'd once been. He couldn't move and he realised that he too had fallen once more, and perhaps forever, into that lifeless state. He tried to cry out for help but his lips seemed stuck fast. Then he heard a voice behind him.

'Siggy. Siggy.'

His body shook. The whole kitchen quaked. Delft and cutlery rattled and spun from the table. The huge dresser behind Teufel and the guard began to keel over and he was sure it would fall on all of them and reduce them to dust for all of eternity.

'Siggy. Siggy,' the voice called again.

Still he couldn't move. The dresser swayed forward and buried Teufel, Wagner and the table in a dense cloud of dry ashes that spun like a million stars before his eyes.

'Siggy. Siggy.'

Siegfried sat up and rubbed his eyes as if to clear away the dream-dust from them.

'Siggy.'

He turned and there, at his side, knelt Dieter, woken from his slumber by Siegfried's fear.

'Would someone like to tell me what's happening here?'

Siegfried woke Anna from her curious encounter with Greta, and for what seemed like hours the three companions talked. There was a lot of explaining to do and Siegfried went about it slowly, trying to make it simple enough for Dieter to understand.

'Siggy, you're talking to me like I was a four-year-old. Like we're still in that dumb book.'

'I'm sorry. It's the way he makes you stutter and....'

'And because someone has a stutter they're supposed to be stupid? And, by the way, you may not have noticed but I don't have a stutter.'

'How could I let myself think like that?'

'The power of words, Siggy. People can be made to believe anything with words.'

Only then did Siegfried notice that Dieter was using his nickname all the time and it didn't matter. That was just another daft notion in Gott's words. He felt no foolish pride in his name; that was all a fantasy in an old man's mind.

If Dieter was, in body, just like he was in the books, with his small stature and one arm, in mind he was very different. In fact, looking at those brown-speckled eyes, Siegfried got the impression that Dieter understood more than he himself did.

'We get to be free but there's a price to pay, right?'

When Dieter said things like this he didn't do so in desperation. There was always a hint of a smile on his impish face, as if he was constantly aware of a funny side to this thing called life.

The typewriter in Herr Gott's room started up too soon, but Dieter didn't panic. He stood up and with his one, strong hand helped Anna to her feet.

'You're actually better-looking here than in the book, do you know that?'

'Dieter!'

Anna wasn't sure what to make of Dieter any more, but his smile was so mischievous that she knew there was no romantic intention on his part.

'Hey,' he added, 'you look great in the book too!'

Even as they drifted towards the Leiningen archway, Siegfried felt something new had entered the stagnant atmosphere of the Grey Room. Things would never seem so awful again now that they had Dieter to lighten their terrible burden with his good humour.

'And Siggy. I've had a cut knee, a grazed elbow and a black eye so far in this story. Don't be too hard on me, right!'

A joke. But like everything Dieter said, as Siegfried had already begun to discover, it betrayed an uncanny grasp of the truth — and the future.

THE LAST
OF THE
LINGEN GANG

PART 5

The night sky over Leiningen, though clouded over, is bright with flickering red and yellow light that can mean only one thing. From the road approaching the village Siegfried scours the skyline and sees at once where the glow is coming from. The Castle is on fire.

'My trinket box!' he gasps. 'The petrol can lid!'

He races through the outskirts of the village, into the fields beyond and through the vast thicket of pine trees that stands like a protective cloak around the old ruins. He hears cries and indignant shouts, and for a moment he thinks he's once more about to confront the terrorists. But when he emerges from the pine-needle-covered path, the first person he sees is Herr Hempel.

The flames have begun to subside. A great ball of smoke rises from the singed mass of ivy on the Castle walls.

'Let's go and get Matthias — now!' someone calls, but another voice asks more uncertainly, 'Why would they want to burn the Castle? What's the point? It's just a pile of stones.'

Of all those present only Siegfried knows the answer to this question. The crowd begins to gather around Herr Hempel, looking to him as always for direction in their confusion. He raises his hands to quell their mutterings.

'Please, calm down. We must have order!'

Siegfried, as yet unnoticed by the others, circles to the rear of the Castle and climbs towards the entrance to the cellars. The smoke, though not as dense as that ascending from the ivy outside, sets his eyes streaming as he goes down the cellar steps. It's so difficult to breathe that he'll have very little time. And then there is the blinding darkness.

He moves through the familiar spaces of the outer room and feels his way to the real Gang room. He reaches out to pull back the hemp curtain but it's gone. Burnt, no doubt. Or merely torn away by the fire-raisers?

Inside the Gang room he's unable to stop himself from coughing. It's too late to turn back and he can only hope that those outside haven't heard him. He stumbles across the wreckage on the floor and reaches into the corner where the set of bookshelves should be. In a frenzy of panic he realises that this too has collapsed. He feels around desperately for the gold-painted trinket box.

Now he can't catch so much as a whiff of breath. He gags and retches and he's aware that in a matter of seconds he may faint. Then his left hand wraps itself around the little metal box. It's as hot as burning coal. He sweeps off his shirt, tearing away every last button in his hurry, and bundles it around the box. He turns and makes for the archway, no longer able to think, hardly able to move.

Somehow he finds the outer room and throws himself at the upward steps, but they come too soon. He goes crashing down and feels a smooth, hard wedge of stone crack against his forehead. He screams and as he drifts away into unconsciousness he's sure the scream hasn't left his lips.

'Siegfried! Are you all right, Siegfried?'

He opens his stinging eyes, but the pain is so bad he has to screw them tightly shut again.

'My box,' he mutters weakly. 'Where's my box?'

At his side, Herr Dielen the blacksmith sighs with relief after his exertions. Dragging Siegfried, a big fellow for his age, up those cellar steps was not easy.

'Over here!' Herr Dielen calls. 'It's young Geistengel!'

In an avalanche of sound the crowd is around Siegfried and he tries once more to force his eyelids apart. Herr Hempel stands above him looking perplexed.

'What were you doing in there?' he asks.

'It's our ... it was ... our Gang room,' Siegfried explains, his voice wheezy from the smoke. 'I had to get the box.... my box ... Where is it?'

Herr Hempel stoops down and from behind Siegfried picks up the small metal casket.

'Is this the one?'

Siegfried is unspeakably happy in spite of the cold that's sending shivers through him. Herr Hempel hands the box to the blacksmith, takes off his overcoat and places it over Siegfried's bare shoulders.

'Open it. See what's inside,' Siegfried says, basking in the warmth of the coat and the prospect of Herr Hempel's praise. The Stationmaster won't be pleased that he's kept the evidence to himself for too long, but it's better late than never, Siegfried thinks.

'Under the shells and things, you'll find it.'

Herr Dielen raises the lid of the box reverently and his look of surprise makes Siegfried feel positively elated. The feeling is short-lived.

'It's empty.'

Siegfried sits up and grabs the box from the blacksmith's work-hardened hands. There's no mistake. The shells, the chestnuts, the coins are gone — and the petrol can lid too. The expressions on the faces around him change from expectation to puzzlement and finally to impatient derision.

'Damn fool boy, wasting our time,' is their verdict as they begin to disperse, leaving only Herr Hempel at his side.

Siegfried wants to crawl away into the nearest crevice in the Castle walls and hide his shame. As people often do in such situations, he begins to look for others to blame. Only Greta knew about the petrol can lid. Had she seen him put it in the trinket box? Was it possible she'd let the vital information slip, perhaps by accident? The very thought is as preposterous as it is unworthy. Maybe Anna or Dieter was snooping around and found the thing. Yes, that seems more likely, but it doesn't make him feel any better. How could he have been so stupid as to hide it there in the first place, he thinks? There's no way around it. The blame lies squarely on his own shoulders.

'I have a confession to make,' he says. Herr Hempel's jaw drops.

Siegfried guesses what the Stationmaster must be thinking.

'Not that kind of confession. I didn't burn the Village Hall or this place.'

Herr Hempel shows such concern and understanding, as Siegfried tells him everything, that the terrible weight of guilt lessens with every word. When Siegfried can find no more to say, Herr Hempel considers the matter in silence for a while. Then he speaks in his usual gentle but firm manner.

'You've done well, Siegfried,' he says. 'But I think you know now you'd have done even better if you'd confided in me earlier.'

'The Hitler Youth will never have me now, will they?' Siegfried asks, expecting the worst.

Herr Hempel helps Siegfried to his feet and smiles.

'We all make mistakes, it's only human,' he asserts. 'The important thing is to learn from those mistakes. I believe you've done that.'

'So I *can* join?'

'Come to my office first thing in the morning, Siegfried. I'll bring the forms.'

Siegfried is overjoyed but feels he doesn't deserve such happiness.

'We might have had Matthias by now if I hadn't been so foolish.'

'Don't worry yourself on that account,' Herr Hempel declares confidently. 'The Jew will soon make *his* mistake. And when he does we shall be waiting.'

In spite of the throbbing in his bruised forehead and the vile taste of smoke catching in his throat, Siegfried walks with a lighter step than he has for days. Nothing, he thinks, can change this glorious new mood of his — but he's quite wrong.

At the hayloft he finds Dieter sleeping. His one hand lies open on the heavy blanket. On the palm of his hand lies the petrol can lid.

'I f-found it here in th-the hay!'

Siegfried searches his mind and can't place the lid anywhere but in the trinket box.

'Dieter? Are you sure you found it here?'

'C-course I am,' Dieter says, and adds tearfully, 'You d-don't believe me, d-do you?'

'Did you tell them about our Gang room?'

'T-tell who?'

'You know who I mean.'

Dieter is becoming frightened. Of what, Siegfried is not quite sure.

'Oh, th-them, the ones who b-beat me up. No! I wouldn't d-do that. I l-love the G-Gang.'

'There's no Gang, not any more,' Siegfried tells the one-armed boy.

Dieter pleads but Siegfried knows he mustn't listen, no matter how desperate the cripple becomes. Siegfried is learning a very necessary lesson. He's learning that a time comes when you have to harden your heart, a time when you have to be cruel to be kind. Dieter may have been misled by others, but he's still guilty.

Finally, Dieter gives up his futile protests. Slipping on his weathered boots — cast-offs from his uncaring father — he stares like a wounded animal at Siegfried.

'Tell your friends,' Siegfried says calmly. 'We're on to them.'

'I have n-no f-friends now,' Dieter answers, and slinks away into the night.

Next morning Siegfried is awake and down in the farmyard before the cock crows for the second time. His father, silent as usual at this hour, soon appears and they set about the early morning chores that keep a well-run farm ticking over. At half past six his mother calls from the kitchen and they have breakfast. The expectant hush of the farmhouse thrills Siegfried and he can wait no longer to make his announcement.

'I'm meeting Herr Hempel at the Station this morning,' he says. The dreamy look in his parents' eyes turns to one of wonder. 'I'm joining the Hitler Youth!'

At seven o'clock he sprints down the lane, ignoring their good-humoured advice that it's a little early to find Herr Hempel at his desk. He continues on his way, thinking, 'I've already waited too long to do the right thing.'

A TWIST IN THE TALE

The Grey Room spun slowly into focus before Siegfried. His forehead ached and he was surprised to feel such real, vivid pain from a fall in that fantasy world of Leiningen. The cruelty he'd shown towards Dieter, though it wasn't his own fault, hurt even more. He turned to find Dieter and was relieved to see him shrug his shoulders as if to say, 'Forget what happened in the story — it's just the ravings of an old fool.'

Anna looked disappointedly at where Greta sat alone at the dusty table.

'I'm so afraid for her. What if we scupper this book before she wakes? What will become of her then?'

'It won't happen like that,' was all Siegfried could say.

He held out little hope for Greta. Their plan to switch chapters would work quickly or not at all. If it did work then Greta would be condemned to remain forever in the Grey Room. He was more certain than ever that once the book was abandoned he and Dieter and Anna would finally become fully real. How could they be expected to live out their lives in this dismal place? Some cruel choices would soon have to be made, and Siegfried didn't want even to begin making them.

'Maybe we should wait for Greta to come round.'

Dieter was quietly insistent. 'No, Siegfried. We have to make things happen. If we try, if we do the best we can, then luck will be on our side — and on Greta's.'

'I think Greta needs a little more than luck,' Anna said dryly.

'Maybe so. But what she doesn't need is all three of us sitting here doing nothing. Just imagine what would happen if we did that and Gott finished the book. Can't you see that we'd soon begin to hate her? For the rest of our lives — no, for the rest of our miserable grey existences — we'd hate her just because we waited for things to happen instead of getting off our backsides and doing something.'

No further words were needed to decide their next move. Wherever Axel was hiding, that same archway would find him. They went through and found themselves in a large hall-like room that was lined on both sides with beds and filled with the smell of pipe tobacco. The place was dark but for the light of the moon shining through four long windows.

On the beds lay old men and young, all clearly very poor judging by the ragged clothes and coats in which they slept. Only one man sat up in his bed. At first, Siegfried didn't recognise the shaven-headed vagabond who was busily scrawling with a worn old pencil on long sheets of brown paper.

The man looked up as if sensing their presence and they saw at once that it was Axel. He raised a finger to his lips and beckoned them to follow him. The passageway between the beds seemed endless and Siegfried was terrified lest any of the other men should see his shadow move stealthily into sight as he passed each of the long windows. An old tramp, whose snow-white beard was brown near the mouth from chewed tobacco, stirred. He seemed for a terrible instant to stare at Siegfried's frozen silhouette on the floor. But the danger passed and the old man turned his face into the pillow and continued his blissful snoring.

When they got through the door Siegfried found that Axel was looking at him very strangely. Anna closed the door on the ragged sleepers.

'Siegfried! I can see you. Very faintly but ... Good God, I can see you!'

It should have been a great moment for Siegfried but instead it was simply frightening. If he was now visible to the human eye then time was running out quickly for their plan — and for Greta.

'You're just as I'd imagined you,' Axel exclaimed. 'But what am I saying — of course you are. I made you!'

'Excuse me,' Dieter piped up. 'Can we get on with it, please?'

Axel jerked his head to where the voice had come from. 'Dieter?'

'At your service. You're smaller than I thought you'd be, and I have to say the haircut is a bit drastic.'

Axel's dumbfounded look gave way to a huge chuckle. Gathering his wits about him, he pointed up a stairway and, still smiling to himself, went up three steps at a time. They followed him to a small office which contained a sturdy metal filing cabinet, a desk, a chair and little else. On the desk was a typewriter where a blank sheet fluttered lazily.

Axel pulled back the chair, sat before the typewriter and looked up at a pretty cuckoo clock on the wall. Siegfried thought it so strangely out of place in the sparsely-furnished room that he took no notice of the time it told.

'We should get down to work. Tell me everything that's happened so far and try to remember even the smallest detail. The small details are the important ones.'

'Are we safe here, Axel?' Anna wondered. 'What kind of place is this?'

'It's a workhouse. We cut logs and get a bed, a bowl of coffee and some black bread in exchange. The monks who run it ask no questions as long as we do our bit.'

Siegfried wasn't convinced.

'What about the other men? Haven't they asked why you're so bruised and all?'

'They've got their own troubles. Now, who's going to give me the story?'

Between the three of them, Anna, Dieter and Siegfried recounted Herr Gott's twisted fable. Time and again it was Anna who came up with the missing bits and pieces Axel was so anxious to hear. He felt sure that among these he would find some way to turn the story round.

As Axel considered the options open to him, the wooden cuckoo popped out and gave a mechanical squawk that made them all jump.

'Quarter to eleven!' Siegfried cried. 'Teufel will be back at Herr Gott's room at eleven.'

Axel's confidence was shaken but he tried to stay calm. As a writer he'd never had a deadline like this before.

'Nice of you to tell me, Siegfried,' he said.

'I'm sorry, everything's happening so quickly and ...'

'It's too late to write a whole chapter. I'm going to have to add a bit to the end of Gott's last chapter instead.'

Anna foresaw a problem.

'What if he's finished typing halfway up the page? A new page is not going to look right, is it?'

'We can tear the page off wherever he finished,' Dieter suggested. 'It'll look messy but Herr Gott isn't exactly very tidy anyway, is he?'

'Right,' Axel said. 'Give me five minutes. I've got an idea.'

For once, they went willingly to the Grey Room and beyond to the unreal world of Leiningen.

~

Axel began to type, hesitantly at first, and then with a passion that knew no obstacle. The words fell like a light life-giving rain on the parched desert of his mind.

~

Within minutes Siegfried is standing breathlessly outside Herr Hempel's locked-up office. Impatiently, he kicks at some loose pebbles on the platform and watches as they spin away onto the railway tracks and beyond. One last pebble waits to be dispatched. Without thinking he whacks it, not towards the tracks but in the direction of the store beside Herr Hempel's office.

Watching the pebble's ascending arc of flight, Siegfried sees disaster has struck long before the glass shatters. Has he finally, he wonders, with one reckless act, put paid to his chances of joining the Hitler Youth? He's tempted to run away before Herr Hempel arrives, which will be any minute now. But if he's seen running that will surely be the end of all his hopes.

No! He must stay. Perhaps he can invent some lie about finding the window broken when he got to the Station. But lying is against his nature and he resolves to present Herr Hempel with the truth, no matter how damning it might be.

He approaches the store dismally and stares at the few glass shards that still cling to the window frame. At once, his gaze is drawn inwards beyond the frame. On the floor of the store, a new silvery petrol can lies as if discarded in a great hurry. Instinctively his hand goes to his pocket and he takes out the petrol can lid from the Village Hall. The can seems, even from this distance, a better match for the engraved lid than the rusty old thing in Matthias's shed. Is it possible that one of Herr Hempel's railway workers is among the conspirators?

He tries the door of the store and to his surprise finds it's not bolted. He steps inside, listening for the slightest sound from the platform. No sound comes.

The can smells strongly of petrol. The lid is a perfect fit. He looks at the initials again and then it hits him like a blow in the stomach.

When he read those initials at the Village Hall he was already convinced of Matthias's guilt. Now he looks closer. 'K', yes, he is quite sure of that still. But the other letter is not and never has been 'M'. He sees clearly now that it's a badly-formed but very definite 'H'.

And he knows too well that Herr Hempel's Christian name is Kurt.

~

No sooner had they returned from Leiningen than Siegfried was speeding back to Axel in the workhouse. It seemed an awfully long time since he'd been there earlier, certainly more than the five minutes Axel had promised. Pulling the sheet from the typewriter, Axel was amazed at how quickly Siegfried had got back to him. Siegfried saw the clock and grabbed the sheet from Axel's hand. Four minutes to eleven!

'You said five minutes.'

'Sorry, I got a bit carried away. It's been so long.'

Siegfried was gone before Axel finished speaking. Back in the Grey Room he called to Dieter and Anna, 'Let's go,' and they passed through the archway to Herr Gott's haven of faded splendour.

~

The old writer was sitting at his desk, his arm stretched out over the pile of typed pages, his head perched uncomfortably on the arm-rest of the chair. To their relief they saw that his eyes were closed, though his sleep was troubled. His tired face seemed to have aged even more. He looked to Siegfried like someone whose life was ebbing away with each uneasy breath.

Yet it was impossible to feel any sympathy for the old man. He had made his pact with the devil, and he was paying the price. Once Axel's page was added to his latest chapter there was no knowing how high that price might be. Whatever it was, as far as Siegfried was concerned, it was no more than Gott deserved.

Dieter pointed to some sheets of paper which lay on the desk on the other side of the typewriter from where Herr Gott's arm was spread. On the top sheet, a heading was plain to be seen. 'The Last of the Lingen Gang — Part 5.'

Siegfried flicked through to the last page and found that luck was, incredibly, on their side again. The words ended on the last line of the page. He deftly added Axel's page to the folded sheets.

In the distance, a cathedral bell tolled the hour and Herr Gott's head rolled from the arm-rest of the chair. Dieter and Anna pressed themselves against the wall but for them there was no immediate danger, both being as yet invisible. For Siegfried it was a different matter. As Herr Gott suddenly sat upright, Siegfried looked desperately for a hiding place. In one movement he was away from the old man's side and rolling under the big canopied bed.

Herr Gott called timidly towards the door.

'Who's there?'

A loud knock had him stumbling from the chair. Dieter and Anna, though they knew this man had brought evil to Leiningen, couldn't help but pity him. They had never seen anything like the mask of sheer terror his face had become. As he braced himself to face his tormentors, Herr Gott pulled his worn woollen cardigan tightly around him as if the threadbare material could offer some protection from

Teufel's blows. From the loose pocket of the cardigan a letter fell, unnoticed by the frightened old man, to the floor.

In his hide-away under the bed Siegfried saw Anna reach out and take the letter while Herr Gott half-ran, half-fell across to the door.

'Sorry to keep you waiting, Herr Haupsturmfuhrer. It's my old legs, you see, not what they used to be.'

The very air splintered like crushed ice when Teufel entered the room. The mirror-black boots advanced. Herr Gott's torn carpet slippers retreated. The chair by the desk was dragged back and Teufel's crossed legs came into Siegfried's view. He spoke in a bitter tone of controlled rage.

'Axel Hoffen escaped last night.'

'Axel? Hoffen? Do I know him?'

'The reptilian creature who wrote the Lingen Gang books, you idiot. Axel bloody Hoffen.'

Herr Gott staggered backwards to the bed. His feet were now within inches of Siegfried's head.

'What does this mean ... for me ... for this book?'

'You'll be finishing the book. I won't be made to look a fool before my superiors.'

'But without Hoffen ...'

'Hoffen or no Hoffen, I *will* see this garbage in print. This business of Hoffen touring the schools and all, we can do without. No, I intend to dispose of him at the first opportunity. In fact, I've already written his obituary for the *Volkische Beobachter, our* newspaper. All very sad really, a dreadful car crash, you know. But fortunately there will be this manuscript found in his possession. *The Last of the Lingen Gang*. Hoffen's reputation will be restored. Can't you just see the impact it will have? Every child in the country will want to read it. There's nothing better than an early death to make a hero of a man ... or even a piece of slime like Hoffen.'

'And if he manages to ... to get out of Germany?'

'He won't. Our spies are everywhere. It's simply a matter of time. Now, let's see if you've taken heed of my advice.'

Siegfried waited for the explosion of anger that was sure to come. One phrase echoed in his mind. 'Our spies are everywhere.' Even among those bedraggled occupants of the workhouse? Axel would have to move on from there and keep moving until he reached the borders of this country that was consumed by devotion to its Führer, Adolf Hitler.

'What in the name of.... What's the meaning of this?'

'The meaning of what?'

'The end of this chapter, you fleabag, all this stuff about Hempel!'

Teufel flung the pages at Herr Gott and they fell right before Siegfried's eyes. One page fluttered inward and came to rest on his hand. Axel's page. He drew back as Herr Gott's trembling hands reached down to gather the sheets. Siegfried's heart no longer seemed to be beating as he moved Axel's page within reach of the grubby fingers. The old man picked it up and within seconds the other pages had fallen again.

'I ... I didn't ....'

'You didn't what?'

'I ... I didn't ....'

Teufel leapt to his feet and made for the old man.

'Have you gone completely mad? Of all the writers I could have had, I had to go and choose a doting old fool. Herr Hempel, the leader of the community, the symbol of all that's right in National Socialism, is now the villain of the piece, is this true?'

'No, no, it's not like that. You see ... this, you see ... is just ... just a little twist in the tale ... to keep the reader interested, you see.'

'A twist?'

Siegfried could almost hear Herr Gott's old mind lurching for an escape from this trap.

'Yes, a twist. You see, young readers, all readers for that matter, like these unexpected things to happen because ... because a story gets stale. But they'll discover in the next chapter that ... that Herr Hempel is really a good German ... that he's been set up by ... by this Jew, Matthias, the real criminal.'

Teufel didn't answer immediately. He began to pace the room in his now-familiar way. Siegfried waited for the Haupsturmfuhrer's decision. Whatever Gott was, he was no doting old fool. He'd covered his tracks well. If he'd blurted out the truth — that he hadn't written this chapter ending — then Teufel would certainly have concluded that the old man was insane.

'It had better be good, this twist of yours. I had thought I might pass the writing of this book to some other greedy hack, but I've changed my mind.'

'Thank you, Herr Haups....'

'Shut up. I haven't changed my mind because you're any damn good. I've had it up to here with this book. If you can't finish it satisfactorily, it won't be finished.'

In the silence that followed, Siegfried sensed that Teufel was having a change of heart about this whole business.

'In fact, I'm beginnining to wonder whether my superiors might be just as pleased to receive two corpses instead of a measly book. Especially if those were the corpses of two miserable writers.'

Herr Gott was on his knees.

'Please, Herr Haupsturmführer, give me one last chance. I need this money.'

'We all need money, Gott.'

'But I want to write this book for the Führer. You've read my words. Haven't I praised him at every turn? Do you imagine I could invent such devotion? How can you prevent me from doing my duty to Adolf Hitler? A man like you who's sworn allegiance to the Great One?'

Teufel considered the genuflecting old man and sighed in exasperation.

'All right, Gott. One last chance. But if you fail, you'll be sorry you ever lived to meet me.'

He swivelled on his heels, delivered a curt 'Heil Hitler' to which Herr Gott replied eagerly, and left.

Siegfried's plan had failed. The book hadn't been abandoned; even now, Herr Gott was trundling across to the typewriter to write himself and Herr Hempel out of the trap Axel had set for them. The old man had to be stopped, no matter what it took.

'No matter what it took.' Siegfried's blood ran cold. Was he prepared to go as far as Teufel, perhaps further, to keep Herr Gott from the typewriter? Siegfried refused to answer his own question, refused to listen to his own protests. Even as he did, he knew that this was all it took to become one of 'them', one of the black or brown-uniformed ones he so despised.

When Siegfried emerged from his hiding place, Herr Gott had already sat down at his desk and was winding a page onto the typewriter.

'Don't do it. Please, listen to me, Herr Gott.'

The old man, wracked with a convulsive tremor, peered into the ill-lit gloom behind him and gasped.

'Who are you? How did you get in here?'

'You know who I am.'

At the side of the desk Anna was beckoning to Siegfried. He ignored her.

'No, I don't. I'll call the guard, I will ... I'll call the guard,' cried Gott.

'And tell him what? That you've seen the ghost of Siegfried Geistengel — a boy in a book?'

Herr Gott turned to his desk and blocked his ears. Siegfried sprang at him and grabbed the old man's hands.

'Listen to me. You know what you're doing is wrong. And if you don't put a stop to it then I'll ... I'll kill you!'

Herr Gott fell to the floor and lay there with his head buried under his arms. Siegfried's eyes, lit by a cold fury, scanned the desk for a weapon and settled on a sharp six-inch letter opener in the form of an Oriental dagger. His hand reached for its cold handle.

Suddenly Anna's hand was on his. In her other hand she held out the letter Herr Gott had dropped earlier.

'Read this.'

He tried to avoid her eyes, not to lose the hate from his own. She insisted.

'Read it.'

He took the letter. For a while, he found it difficult to make sense of the old writer's fragile handwriting.

'Dearest daughter Romi,' the letter began, 'I hope this note finds you safe and well. Don't worry yourself on my account. Why, I've never been so healthy in all my life. Every evening I walk along Unter Den Linden and meet my old friends at the Blue Note Café. No wine, mind you, just good South American coffee. Better still, I've found a way, at last, to get the money to help you and Chaim to escape this sad country.

'One of these old friends, you see, has asked me to do a spot of ghost-writing. Very simply, it means writing an "autobiography" for a film actor (whose name I can't tell you now, you understand). The thing is that this fellow has very little between his ears and couldn't write his own name. So I do the job, and when it's finished he'll pretend he's written it and I'll collect a fat cheque — enough to take all of us to safety.

'I can't tell you how much I regret the pain I've put you through since you married Chaim. Did I see in him a man, loving and kind? Did I see the doctor working among the poor? No. I looked at Chaim and saw only a Jew. I know how much it must have hurt you — and your poor departed mother — when I refused even to see your children. I've been foolish and cruel and don't deserve your love. Perhaps now I can undo some of the harm I've done.

'I ask you to accept this money when it comes, as I swear it will. This time I will not fail you, my daughter. I will send you the money if it is the last thing I do.

'Your undeserving father,

'Hans.'

Siegfried bent down and tried to lift the old man from his cowering position. Herr Gott resisted stubbornly.

'Go away. Just go away.'

'We'll get the money for Romi some other way,' Siegfried pleaded — though quite how or where, he had no idea. 'Only don't write this awful book.'

The old man pushed Siegfried aside. Siegfried was so surprised that he stumbled back, and before he recovered, it was too late to stop Herr Gott from reaching the keys of the typewriter. Neither Dieter nor Anna had the strength yet to intervene.

'You should have let me kill him!' was the last thing Siegfried remembered saying before the Leiningen sun once more blazed into his mind.

THE LAST
OF THE
LINGEN GANG

PART 6

'Think!' Siegfried tells himself. 'Think! Think!'

There must be an explanation for this. It makes no sense, no sense whatsoever, that Herr Hempel could have burnt the Village Hall or the Castle or tried to set the school alight. It can only be ... it can only be ...Yes! A plot! A cynical plot of Matthias's to make the villagers doubt Herr Hempel's great leadership. That must be it, he thinks, that must be it. What lengths these people will go to destroy the village's peace!

He studies the engraved letters on the underside of the petrol can lid. A 'K' certainly. But an 'M'? Or an 'H'? And now it comes to him. He laughs aloud at his own stupidity and the ridiculous conclusion he jumped to. This is no carelessly scrawled 'H' but a blatant, ham-fisted attempt to change the letter 'M'. And who would want to do that but the bearer of that initial — Matthias!

The sun streaming in the open door warms his back and, inside, he feels a similar warm glow of relief. Suddenly he's covered in a blanket of shadow. He stands up slowly and faces the door.

'Thank heavens, it's you!'

'Who did you think it was?' Herr Hempel asks evenly. 'Do you want to tell me what's going on?'

'I do, Herr Hempel. I'm sorry about the window but you'll be glad I ... I broke it when you hear.'

Siegfried is right for once. Herr Hempel is more than glad to hear of his discovery.

'Yes, just as I thought,' he nods sagely. 'Matthias is beginning to panic. The noose is tightening around his neck and he doesn't like it, not one little bit. Leave this to me, Siegfried. Matthias will soon be ours to deal with as we choose.'

'Isn't there anything I can do?'

Herr Hempel rolls the petrol can in his palm and Siegfried can see he's thinking hard but coolly.

'Perhaps there is,' the Stationmaster tells him. 'Yes, I believe there is. It seems to me that either Anna or Dieter or perhaps both, in fact almost certainly both, are part of this conspiracy. I think you suspect this too?'

Siegfried has to agree. It has been his own instinct from the very start. If there is any doubt left in his mind on the matter, it is soon shattered by Herr Hempel's keen detecting skills.

'You were certain that this initial was an M before you put it in the trinket box, am I right?'

'Yes.'

'And when it was returned to you — and only then — you were unsure?'

'That's right.'

'And who, let us say, "found" the lid in your father's hayloft?'

'Dieter!' Siegfried exclaims. 'That means ...'

Herr Hempel smiles patiently as Siegfried tumbles to the truth.

'That means that either Dieter changed the initial or someone else did and Dieter was given the job of returning it to me.'

'The cripple is the weak link in their scheme, Siegfried. If my instinct is right he'll point the finger at Matthias — without, perhaps, quite naming him. If you can get him to confess, I'll do the rest.'

'I'll go this very minute, Herr Hempel,' Siegfried promises faithfully.

'I've spoken to your father about this boy. When this business has been sorted out I'll have him despatched to a Home for the Criminally Insane. At least in there he won't be used by the likes of Matthias. Now, I've something for you to sign.' The Stationmaster fishes a brown envelope from his pocket and opens it.

The Hitler Youth registration forms! Bursting with pride, Siegfried writes his heroic name in his best copperplate script, which isn't easy to do given his state of high excitement. Herr Hempel pockets the forms and offers his hand to Siegfried.

'Welcome,' he says, 'to the Führer's young army. Tonight at eight you're to be sworn in.'

Siegfried doesn't know what to say. He's so filled with emotion that he's beyond words.

'There's no need to say anything. Your face says it all,' Herr Hempel reassures him. 'Now go and talk to Dieter — and Anna too. Take it as your first Hitler Youth task. And remember, the time for gentle persuasion has passed.'

Siegfried has never hit Dieter before. There have been times when he's been sorely tempted. He's always resisted in spite of all the plans the cripple has messed up, all the adventures that came close to catastrophe because of his sheer stupidity. But this is no mere adventure and Dieter's refusal to answer Siegfried's question has nothing to do with stupidity.

'P-please, S-Siggy ... Siegfried. D-don't hit me again.'

'Answer me! These terrorists didn't really beat you up, did they? No! You fell coming back through the fields like you always do, didn't you?'

He strikes out again. He realises that it gets easier, this business of interrogation, once you get over your weak-minded sympathy for those who don't deserve mercy. He feels strong, proud that his childish softness has disappeared.

Dieter gives in. He nods. Yes, it was just a fall, not a beating.

'And you know who they are, don't you?'

'Th-they had hoods on. I t-told you, Si —'

'One of them has a beard, Dieter,' Siegfried yells.' 'Am I right?'

Dieter scrambles back towards the ditch where the Lingen River flows gently by.

'M-maybe I saw a b-beard sticking out under the b-bottom of the m-mask,' he whines.

Just as Herr Hempel predicted, Dieter has all but admitted it was Matthias. What Dieter has said is the closest to a confession Siegfried can expect. He has taken enough craven stuttering from the cripple. He aims a kick at the ragged-trousered backside and Dieter falls helplessly into the shallow stream.

'Herr Hempel will get the truth out of you — before he sends you to the kind of place where you belong.'

'I'm going to d-drown. Help me! Help me!'

Siegfried laughs and walks away. Even a rat, he tells himself bitterly, can't drown in three inches of water.

His conversation with Anna is as brief and pointless as he'd expected. It doesn't bother him. Her guilt is as clear to him as the water in the Lingen River — if not as pure.

'You know what your father has been up to,' he says flatly.

Anna tries one of her sickly-sweet smiles on him. It doesn't work.

'You live in the same house,' he continues. 'Unless you're blind or stupid you must know.'

She forces a pearly tear to flow down her dark face. Another failed trick.

'I gave you every chance,' he concludes. 'But, you Jewish swine, the game is up and you can tell that sick-minded father of yours I said so.'

He feels quite calm as she runs away cursing him loudly with blasphemies no decent girl should know. That sense of calm remains all afternoon and into the evening. Then, an hour before his first Hitler Youth meeting, it is overturned by a veritable storm of wonder and excitement. The cause of this change is his parents' unexpected gift to him, presented bashfully by his young brother, Max.

'What's this?' Siegfried asks as the little blond boy holds up the brown paper parcel. It reminds him of the one Herr Hempel brought for his father.

He tears the parcel open. It's not a time to act like a child, but he could weep with joy and gratitude. A Hitler Youth uniform! The light brown shirt, the fine leather belt. And here, the tie, and the crisply-ironed trousers.

'I'll make you proud of me,' he chokes. 'I really will, I'll make you proud of me.'

'We always have been,' his father says, as his mother dabs a tear from her eye. 'And always will be.'

~

Siegfried's initiation into the glorious ranks of the Hitler Youth is all he imagined it might be and more. As if walking into a dream, he enters a large hall full of uniformed boys. They're listening to Hans Stiefel, a classmate of Siegfried's, who's reading aloud a story about the old Germanic Gods: the story — and this is in honour of their new member — of the mythical fighter Siegfried, slayer of dragons, merciless persecutor of evil in all its forms.

When Hans has finished speaking, the People's Radio Receiver is switched on and they listen in awe to the voice of Adolf Hitler. Siegfried's wonder is all the greater because this is the first time he's ever actually heard that master of the speech-making art.

As soon as the broadcast ends the whole company breaks into the Horst Wessel Song. Horst Wessel was an early colleague of Adolf Hitler in the battle to make Germany great again. He never lived to see his Leader come to power, but his spirit lives on in this sad but hugely uplifting song. Looking around at the slogans painted in bright red on the walls, Siegfried knows that he too is capable of making the ultimate sacrifice for his people, for his country, for his Führer.

'THROUGH THE DOOR OF DEATH WE ENTER THE DOOR OF LIFE,' one slogan reads.

'WE ARE BORN TO DIE FOR GERMANY,' proclaims another.

The moment he's been waiting for arrives. A long black curtain at the far end of the hall is drawn back by two Hitler Youths. Siegfried's name is called ritually by Hans Stiefel.

Siegfried stands up from among the crowd seated on the floor and advances towards the inner sanctum.

Inside, the walls are draped with black cloth upon which is emblazoned the *Siegrune*, a white double flash of lightning, the Hitler Youth emblem. From the ceiling blood-red swastikas hang suspended by chains. Burning candles surround a high altar-like table. Here lie a red and black ribboned wreath; a bullet-dented steel helmet; and a photograph of a Hitler Youth Leader who, like Horst Wessel, died for the cause of a pure Germany.

Siegfried drops to his knees. His face is transfigured by devotion. The ceremony begins.

DEATH OF A WRITER

Siegfried's first thought when he returned to the Grey Room was the same as his last before he'd left it. 'They should have let me kill him.' He could still do it, just as he'd beaten Dieter in the story — except that with Gott he wouldn't stop with a kick in the pants. Violence coursed through his veins. If Anna hadn't woken and gaped at him in such a startled way he might have gone, there and then, and put paid to the old writer.

'What are you gawking at?'

'I've seen that look before,' Anna said.

'I don't know what you're talking about,' he snapped. 'And neither do you.'

'Just now, in the book. When you called me a Jewish swine, you had that look.'

'Those weren't *my* words and you know it. If I'm going to be blamed for the words Gott puts in my mouth then surely it's right to kill him — before he destroys me.'

Dieter woke with a sleepy grin on his face.

'What's all the racket for? A fellow can't even have a nap around here.'

'You shut up!'

Siegfried seemed to crumble then. He fell against the wall and slid down to the grimy floor, bowing his head in shame and fear.

'What's happening to me? I didn't mean to say ...'

Dieter and Anna were frightened too. A silence very like the silence of their long hibernation spread through the Grey Room. They might have been as empty of life as Greta still was. In each of their troubled minds the same awful truth asserted itself. Real life was too difficult. It was so much easier to be a character in a book. When the story pauses you can rest and there is nothing to bother you. And when the book ends you can sleep a sleep without nightmares for months, perhaps years — even, if you're lucky, for all of eternity.

'Let the book end,' they thought as one. 'Let all books end so that we can sleep forever.'

And then — Greta woke.

They were electrified, all three. A new energy, an energy that would have seemed impossible only moments before, charged through them. Greta wanted to know everything and she wanted to know it now — immediately. In the telling, the story of those last few days became an adventure all of its own. When they reached the end, or rather brought the story to where it stood, their earlier hopelessness and despair had given way to a new sense of purpose.

Greta, the icy look of disdain gone from her face, summed up the situation as she saw it.

'So there are two things we have to do now. We have to find the money for Herr Gott's daughter, Romi. And we have to warn Axel to move on before these spies of Teufel's catch up with him.'

'But we have to convince Gott to take the money,' Anna added. 'And we have to convince him that we can help him escape Teufel.'

'That makes four things we have to do,' Dieter interjected. 'Anyone got some more?'

They looked at him, wondering if he was challenging their fresh sense of hope. But Dieter was smiling.

'Only joking. Let's get started. Let's get Axel out of that workhouse. There's something about that place I don't like.'

And so they went to the smoky dormitory to find their true creator. Axel hadn't been able to sleep. He sat with his knees drawn up on the hard bed. Beside him lay another poem scrawled on the same rough brown paper as the other four he'd written since his escape from the prison cell. This latest one, 'Angels Without Wings', seemed to him to finish the sequence. Soon he'd move on to write even better ones. And stories for the young, for the old, for everyone. He had never known such happiness or confidence in his future.

These verses, he'd decided, would be called *Prison Poems (see back of book)*. He looked forward with the writer's childlike eagerness to seeing them in print some day. It was so good to feel optimism again that nothing worried him now. Not the fact that all of Germany was a prison for him, for he would soon be away from it. Nor the possibility that Siegfried's trick might have failed, for he was sure that between them, he and the Gang would come up with something else.

They were next to him before he'd become aware of their presence. He wasn't at all surprised to see Anna's black hair and olive-skinned face beside Siegfried.

Nor was he surprised to hear a fourth voice, Greta's; he was merely relieved that she too had come to life. However, now that he could see Siegfried more clearly among the shadows, he guessed that all had not gone well with the plan.

'It hasn't worked?'

'I'm afraid not. But at least we know that Herr Gott isn't writing this rot because he really believes in it.'

Siegfried went on to explain about the letter they'd found and the urgent need to find money for Gott's daughter,

Romi. As he did so, an old grey-bearded man turned from side to side on his uncomfortable bed at the far end of the room.

'We shouldn't be talking here,' Dieter whispered. 'Isn't that the same fellow who was stirring last time?'

'Don't mind him. The poor chap tosses and turns all night, every night. In the morning he tells me about his nightmares.'

'You didn't tell him who you were, did you?' Anna wondered.

'Of course not.'

'You'll have to leave this place,' Siegfried told him. 'Teufel has spies in every town and village. We heard him say so.'

'I'd planned on leaving tonight in any case. I'm heading for the Polish border and on to Warsaw. There's a publisher I know of there and I want to show him these poems I've written. I feel so good about them ... I feel so good about life.'

They were happy for him in spite of the uncertainty of their own situation — none more so than Siegfried, who'd seen Axel rise from the depths of despair back in that attic room. Axel, in his gratitude, hadn't forgotten the dilemma of the Lingen Gang.

'Sometimes,' he said mysteriously, 'stealing is only taking back what's rightfully yours.'

'What do you mean?' the unseen Greta asked.

'When my books were first banned I knew I'd have to leave Germany. So I went to my bank to take out the money I had there. Not a fortune but not a sum to be sniffed at either. They refused to give it to me, said the authorities were examining my affairs or some such excuse. Ten thousand marks should be enough to satisfy Herr Gott, shouldn't it?'

Dieter almost laughed aloud at the prospect.

'You're suggesting we rob a bank?'

'No. It's even simpler than that. See, I followed the bank clerk who refused me — Herr Gier — followed him to his flat at 27 Richtofenstrasse. While I pleaded with him I saw a pile of money on his table. More money than a mere bank clerk should have. I'm sure it was my money.'

'But what if Herr Gott won't take it?' Anna objected.

'We'll worry about that when the time comes,' Greta said.

Siegfried had a different answer to Anna's question, though he didn't dare say it aloud. If Herr Gott refused to co-operate he would have to kill him. As far as he could see, there was no alternative. In the end, it would be a matter of their lives or his.

'You'd better go now, Axel,' he said, in an effort to put this inescapable fact to the back of his mind.

Axel folded his coarse sheets of paper and stuffed them in the inside pocket of the jacket given to him by the monks. The jacket was a very tight fit and when he'd done up the buttons he grinned broadly.

'I look like Charlie Chaplin!'

In their first adventure the Gang had been to a cinema in a nearby town and seen a Charlie Chaplin film. They remembered that innocent episode with an affection tinged with sadness. It hadn't all been bad in Leiningen, not in those earlier stories.

Dieter, however, was quick to cheer them up.

'You're funny, Axel, but not that funny. Maybe you should stick to the writing.'

'I will,' Axel said with a fierce urgency, 'I really will. And it's all thanks to you lot.'

Axel had nothing in the world but the second-hand clothes he stood in. And yet, with the poems tucked close to his heart, he had everything. They watched him walk lightly from the dormitory into the happy future that beckoned to him and then they turned to go. Siegfried straggled behind the others, absorbed in the terrible choice he might soon be faced with.

A single gunshot blasted him from his reverie. He raced through the ranks of beds to where the sound still reverberated. As he passed, the bearded man — who was not at all old, his beard merely powdered to seem grey — smiled beneath his horse blanket and rolled the thirty-mark reward between his soiled palms.

Leaping down the stairway outside the dormitory, Siegfried reached an outside hallway. At the open front door, Axel Hoffen lay dead.

Siegfried knelt over his creator, shook him, begged him to speak, pleaded with him not to die, but it was too late. Nearby, he heard a shuffling in the darkness and the clicking of a gun preparing to shoot again.

'Hold your fire! He's one of us! A Hitler Youth!'

The voice of Hauptsturmführer Teufel. Only then did Siegfried realise he himself was dressed in the light-brown uniform from the book. 'Never,' he wanted to scream, 'I'll never be one of you, Teufel.' But if he wanted to live to fight another day he must disappear from sight.

'Goodbye, Axel,' he whispered; and then, remembering the words from this latest book, which though they were Gott's said all he wanted to say, 'I'll make you proud of me. I really will. I'll make you proud of me.'

He took the sheaf of poems from Axel's pocket and slipped back into the workhouse. At that precise moment Herr Gott woke in a panic that was worse than anything he'd ever felt before.

Siegfried crossed the echoing hallway and climbed the stairs towards the dormitory. Herr Gott swept back the covers from his bed and rushed to the desk, trying to make his tired mind understand this new, this excruciating fear.

Through the dormitory Siegfried went, and Herr Gott's hands shook so much he couldn't find the keys on the typewriter. The old man heard no footsteps but knew someone was coming to finish him off. Kroll? Teufel? Or the ghost of ...

Siegfried Geistengel reached the Grey Room. Sweat poured like stale wine from Herr Gott's brow. He smelled the whiff of murder in the air and he knew who the murderer was to be. 'Thou shalt not kill,' he told himself. 'Except in self-defence, surely!' He began to type — in self-defence.

THE LAST
OF THE
LINGEN GANG

PART 7

This is the greatest night of Siegfried's life and the sky above Leiningen reflects the glorious feeling inside of him. The moon is full and bigger than he's ever seen it. The stars are brighter and more numerous than on any night ever before. Below, the village itself is breathtakingly beautiful and serene. The silvery shingles of its sloping roofs twinkle like the calmest of night seas. And Siegfried's passage through those streets is as unruffled as some great ocean liner's in untroubled waters.

In the morning he'll tell Herr Hempel of Dieter's admission about a bearded man. Herr Hempel will, as he's promised, 'do the rest'. Together with the evidence of the petrol can lid and the botched attempt to change that initial, there is surely a strong enough case to arrest Matthias. The village will be at peace and its people united in their support of Adolf Hitler and the National Socialist movement.

Such are Siegfried's thoughts as he strides proudly in his Hitler Youth uniform along the low road to the Unterlingen

Farm. Suddenly, an unexpected cloud seems to flit by the moon and momentarily darken the sky. He looks up. There's no cloud; but just above him, on the high grassy bank by the road, are the silhouettes of three men not more than ten yards distant. He turns to run but two hooded figures block his way. A damp hand clamps itself to his mouth and stifles the scream in his throat.

All is in darkness. An old hemp bag has been lowered over his head. He kicks and punches wildly but to no avail against the rope they tie him with. Soon he's carried along by the silent men. He can't be sure in which direction they're taking him but it feels as though he's floating upwards.

The hoarse panting of his abductors convinces him that they're climbing towards Lingen Peak. An unmistakable smell of crushed pine needles follows and, some minutes later, the harsh odour of old smoke is final proof of their destination. The Castle.

He feels himself sinking as they descend into the cellar. They bustle him through the outer room and in the old Lingen Gang room they fling him unceremoniously to the floor. The hemp bag over his head slips back, but the room is pitch dark except for the suggestion of light near the archway. There, one of the abductors stands behind the others. Below his hempen hood Siegfried sees the outline of a beard.

'I know it's you, Matthias. You won't speak because you know I'll recognise your voice!'

One of the others laughs grimly and punches him in the chest before securing the hemp bag with a rough cord around Siegfried's neck. It's difficult to breathe, but he tries to calm himself by working slowly and carefully at the rope tying his hands behind his back. The knot isn't as tight as it first seemed. Given enough time he'll be able to free himself.

'What the hell do we do with him now?'

The shock he feels comes not from the words but from the fact that one of the men has spoken at all. Why, he wonders, has he not recognised the voice? Is it simply that he's been too absorbed with the knot behind his back?

'You know what we have to do,' another says, another stranger.

And, of course, that's it. Some of the Jews of the village are undoubtedly here but, like Matthias, they'll not dare to speak. The ones who do are outsiders. He remembers Herr Hempel talking to the men of the village about the international conspiracy of the Jewish people. Matthias has brought in these strangers to help him with his dirty work. That's what makes these people so dangerous. There are so many of them and in every country in Europe, in the world, they plot and scheme and help each other in their dastardly plan to enslave good people everywhere.

The knot is coming loose. He'll have to draw Matthias away from that archway so that when he makes his burst for freedom the Jew won't be blocking his path. He senses from listening to their short breaths that the others are sitting or crouching around the room. He fixes in his mind exactly where each one is in the familiar space. He gets his hands untied and flexes them for his escape.

'Herr Hempel knows everything, Matthias. You'll be arrested in the morning. You filthy Jew, you stupid filthy Jew, you didn't even have the sense to cover your greasy beard.'

The reaction is not quite what he expects. His captors simply start laughing at him, each one adding an ignorant guffaw until they reach an ear-splitting crescendo. Then Siegfried takes the biggest chance of his young life.

He whips his hands from behind him, tugs away the hood and dives headlong at the archway, punching the hooded Matthias aside. He sprints through the outer room. Bolting up the steps, he lunges towards the square of light above. Feet crunching across the burnt ivy on the Castle floor, he reaches a gap in the outer walls, squeezes through and in one leap is on the forest path.

The branches of trees flash past him and the yells of his pursuers seem more distant with his every step. Then he hears a sound that's like the explosive crack of an axe in an ancient tree. A cold shudder passes through him, beginning somewhere at the back of his head and flowing, sinking down, down along his limbs.

For no reason he can think of, he stops running. He doesn't want to stop. He drops to his knees and stares at the thick tree-trunk before him as if he were searching for the wound in the bark made by that axe. There is no axe, no wound on the tree, and the realisation hits him as the cold pain cuts into the back of his head.

He slumps forward and his lips move as his young body finds its final rest. His words come softly in the quiet wood and he becomes one with the spirit of the ancient trees and the German soil into which his blood seeps.

'We are born,' he whispers, 'to die for Germany.'

NOWHERE TO TURN

'He's really dead, isn't he?'

Only Anna was able to say that dread word. Dead.

They'd been back in the Grey Room for some time now, exactly how long none of them could have guessed. The hero of the Lingen Gang adventures hadn't yet stirred.

'How can we tell for sure? Maybe it's just another twist in Herr Gott's story.'

'If that was true, Dieter, he'd be talking to us now. No, Herr Gott has killed him.'

Beside Dieter, Greta wrapped her cardigan closer and shivered uncontrollably in her light summer dress.

'It's so much colder here now. It feels different somehow.'

Dieter looked around the Grey Room. The atmosphere had certainly changed but it seemed to him that everything else about the room had remained the same. The table and chairs, the bookshelves in the corner, the archways at either end. The archways!

'Anna! Greta!'

The girls turned to him and then followed his gaze. Axel's archway had disappeared.

Greta stood up slowly, thinking aloud as she rose.

'Wherever Axel is, that archway should lead to him. And if it's no longer there then Axel isn't anywhere we can find him ... so he must be ... Oh, my God. Axel is dead too.'

Death in the real world and death in the nightmare world of Leiningen were equally final. With Axel gone there could be no more mischievous twists to undermine Herr Gott's story. With Siegfried gone they were without a leader. They'd always depended on him to come up with a plan or simply to lead by his courageous example. Now, it seemed to them, there was nowhere for them to turn.

'What can we do?' Dieter asked. 'There's no one to show us the way.'

Anna knew that what she had to say wouldn't please the others, but she had to speak.

'Who says we *have* to have a leader? There's no law that says so, only the kind of laws that people like Adolf Hitler dream up. And why? Because they want to be the leaders.'

'I can't believe you're comparing Siegfried to Hitler,' Dieter gasped.

'All I'm saying is that if people depend on a leader, if *we* depend on a leader, to do our thinking for us, then the day will come when we can't think for ourselves.'

Greta was beginning to see the sense in Anna's words. She tried to reassure Dieter.

'We all know Siegfried wasn't like *him*, but then Siegfried never asked to be made into a leader. Axel did that — and no, I'm not blaming Axel either. He wrote the Gang books in the same way that kind of book has always been written. You have a leader, a joker and a couple of none-too-bright girls and the rest is easy.'

'Easy but far from reality,' Dieter said, and felt the weight of despair lifting from his shoulders.

The tense atmosphere lightened and a new urgency entered Anna's voice.

'Everything that's happened to us has been *impossible*. You know, that makes me think that anything, everything is possible.'

Dieter and Greta looked at each other and knew what Anna meant.

'Siegfried,' Greta said.

'We *can* get him back,' Dieter declared. '*Impossible* is only a word.'

It wasn't long before they'd agreed on what to do next.

'Only Herr Gott can bring Siegfried back to life,' Anna said. 'And if he can write a letter like that to his daughter then there's a heart beating in him somewhere and ...'

'... and we can prove to him there's another way to get that money and ...' Dieter added.

'... and we can convince him we'll get him out of Berlin,' Greta concluded.

A pale watery dawn broke through the mist over Berlin. In a poky little upstairs flat on Richtofenstrasse, Herr Gier the moustached bank clerk looked out of his window somewhat disappointedly. Tonight, he and his Brownshirt friends were to stand guard alongside the black-uniformed SS at a celebration of last year's May 10th book-burning on Unter Den Linden. The festivities would take the form of yet another massive bonfire of banned books.

He sighed and considered the wet street outside. He looked on the brighter side of things. A rich man, what with Axel Hoffen's money and the savings of several other artists and writers, he had no cause to feel sorry for himself even on this miserable night. Besides, he thought, it would take more than rain to stop the march of Nazism from which he was profiting so well. Eleven years would pass before he saw the Berlin sky rain fire.

In his once-grand canopied bed, Herr Gott's sleep was far from contented. He dreamt that his daughter Romi, her husband Chaim, and their two beautiful young daughters were all characters in a book written by a madman. They were being chased through a forest and every now and then he could see the crazed writer hunched over his typewriter. He couldn't see the writer's face but, at first, he was sure it was himself as a younger man. Then he thought it was Hauptsturmführer Teufel.

The fatal shots rang out one by one. The girls fell among the pine needles. Then Chaim fell, his arm slung protectively over his daughters.

Sweat poured from Herr Gott's body to the soiled pillow as Romi ran desperately towards a bright clearing ahead. Suddenly he was standing in that very clearing. She was twenty yards, fifteen yards from him, but he was bound hand and foot and couldn't move to help her.

Then the final shot came. Romi staggered. A cry jammed in his throat, cut off by the cord strangling him. In the moment before he woke he saw the face of the mad writer, smiling at him and shouting. His voice was small and tinny as if it came from a radio. The voice, the face were those of Adolf Hitler. The voice cried, 'Hold your fire! He's one of us!'

Herr Gott woke coughing and spluttering as though the cord was still tight around his neck. He opened his eyes to end the terror, but another nightmare awaited him. Around his bed stood Anna, Dieter and Greta, all perfectly visible to him.

'I'm still dreaming. I haven't woken ...'

'You're not dreaming,' Greta told him.

Dieter fought back the urge to hit the old man. Instead, he yelled at him.

'Do you realise what you've done to Siegfried?'

Herr Gott pulled the blankets closer to his chin.

'I've done nothing to anyone. I'm writing a book.'

'Bring him back to life, Herr Gott. You must. You know what love is, you love Romi. We love Siegfried and you've taken him from us.'

Herr Gott buried his face in his hands to block out the vision of Anna's pleading.

'It's because I haven't had a drink in days. This is what happens, you begin to imagine things. You're not real, any of you.'

Anna touched the old man's hands which gripped the edge of the blanket.

'You can feel me touch you. Is that a dream?'

He drew his hands below the blanket and looked out at them again from beneath his grey eyebrows.

'You're not real! How could I have killed a boy who isn't real? A stupid bloody story I never wanted to write — I had to ... had to ... to save ...'

Dieter slammed his fist against the rickety bedboard above the old man's head.

'Right then, Herr Gott. I'll show you what's real!'

The girls looked at him in trepidation and, reading each other's mind, eyed the dagger-shaped letter opener on the writing desk. They moved to hold Dieter back but he was away, not towards the desk but back to the Grey Room. Herr Gott struggled to a sitting position, sensing the girls' confusion.

The one-armed boy swayed back into view again. Over his shoulder lay the body of Siegfried Geistengel. The girls rushed to help him and together they carried Siegfried to the big bed. Such was his terror that Herr Gott was unable to move or cry out even as the fair-haired boy's head fell back on the pillow beside him.

The old man stared at Siegfried and at the folded sheets of brown paper that were halfway out of the breast pocket of his Hitler Youth shirt. Herr Gott reached for them and began to read the *Prison Poems* of Axel Hoffen. Just before the old writer had gone to sleep, the SS guard Kroll had told him of Hoffen's death at Teufel's hands. Even now Kroll was at a nearby tavern celebrating the event.

The old man seemed to grow smaller and weaker at the turn of each page. When he'd finished reading the poems for the second time he laid back his head alongside Siegfried's.

'Last time he spoke to me, Siegfried mentioned money, that he could get this money for Romi.'

The way was clear. Herr Gott was, at last, on their side. Yes, he said, it didn't matter where the money came from. Yes, he would write another chapter where Siegfried would be seen not to be really dead. He only hoped it wasn't too late. And yes, he understood that the book could not end because if it did then the Gang would never be free.

'Give us an hour, Herr Gott,' Dieter said, 'and we'll have Romi's money. Then you can write ....'

'I'll do it now. I know I can trust you.'

He threw back the blanket and in his baggy pyjamas he walked unsteadily to the writing desk. Greta helped him as he faltered yet again on the threadbare carpet.

'Are you all right?'

'I will be. Soon, I'll ...'

He was too weak to continue speaking and when he reached the chair he collapsed heavily into it. His hands trembled above the keys. He's not going to find the strength to type, Dieter thought. Their worst fear — that Herr Gott would die before the words of Siegfried's resurrection were written — seemed possible now.

Greta took the old man's hands in hers and rested them on the typewriter keys.

'I can't go on,' he muttered.

'You must go on,' Greta whispered. 'For Romi and Chaim and the girls — and for Siegfried.'

He began to type, at first one slow letter at a time, then more quickly and more quickly still. Dieter and Anna took hold of Siegfried and raised him from the bed. The old writer didn't even notice them leave, his heart was beating so fast, his mind growing so clear. Everything seemed so simple now he cared not a whit for Teufel's threats. There would be another twist in this Lingen Gang story, he vowed, no matter what the consequences. And another twist in his own.

Herr Hans Gott suddenly knew how the book of his own life would end, and he was happy.

THE LAST
OF THE
LINGEN GANG

PART 8

'Siegfried!' they call. The sound of his name ricochets from tree to tree in the dark wood.

Just moments ago, Dieter and Greta heard the shot. Now, with Siegfried's name echoing away into the distance, a clamour of footsteps approaches them. They dive from the path to the undergrowth and lie quite still, though they're attacked by a thousand pine needles.

'They've got to be here somewhere,' an unfamiliar voice mutters roughly. 'I'm sure it's those Lingen Gang kids.'

'Forget it,' another more commanding voice asserts. 'Let's get out of here.'

Dieter clenches his one fist and from his lips comes a triumphant, whispered 'Yes!' The real terrorists move off down the path towards the village and the wood falls silent again. The voice is well known to both of them and proves that, despite their many doubts, they have been right all along.

They stand up, shake off the clinging pine needles and continue their search.

Around the next curve of the path they find him and are on their knees by him in an instant. Dieter cradles Siegfried's head and feels the blood, wet on his hands.

'No!' he cries. 'No, no! He can't be, he can't be.'

In the passion of his grief he lifts Siegfried and holds him tight. Suddenly he feels a muffled cough deep in his chest and realises it's coming from Siegfried. He releases the prisoner of his affection and from behind him hears Greta's laughter.

'You're choking me, Dieter,' Siegfried yelps.

'I thought you were dead!' Dieter exclaims. 'All that blood and the shot and ...'

'Look beside you,' Greta tells him, stifling another outburst. 'I know I shouldn't be laughing, Siegfried, but ...'

Dieter's and Siegfried's heads turn as one. Before them is a paint tin. Of course! The tin of red paint from the unfinished treehouse. The terrorist's shot obviously dislodged it from above, and when it crashed down on him, Siegfried was knocked cold. The back of his head aches and he feels so downright silly for thinking he'd died for Germany that his sense of relief is of little comfort.

And besides, there are questions to be answered. Why is Dieter here in the first place after their encounter earlier in the day? Why does Greta appear to be so friendly with the one-armed boy? And where is Anna?

The last question is the only one he asks aloud.

'We helped them to escape,' Greta says. 'All of the Matthiases.'

'You *what?*'

Siegfried's head spins wildly as he clambers to his feet, refusing their help with a gruff dismissal. Dieter's benign smile is beginning to annoy him. He looks to Greta for some explanation but her smile is even more annoyingly pleasant.

'Can you walk?' Dieter asks.

'Of course I can walk. I'm not a ...'

'A cripple?'

'What's going on here, Greta?' he shouts. 'You've let those Jews ... those terrorists escape! Why?'

Dieter and Greta swap knowing glances and his nod is an invitation to her to begin the explanation. Siegfried leans against a tree-trunk to steady himself. Strange things are happening in his mind as he stares at them. Somehow, in the blink of an eye, he forgets who they are, only to remember again briefly and once more forget.

'The terrorists have escaped, that's true,' Greta tells him. 'See, they were all outsiders, brought in to work their vicious tricks. All except one, that is.'

'Yeah,' Siegfried says. 'Matthias.'

'Will you come with us?' Dieter pleads. 'If we hurry, you'll understand everything.'

Siegfried clutches his reeling head.

'You're not making sense. Nothing makes any sense.'

'Come with us,' Greta urges him. Remembering how she's always been his ally, he follows.

As they emerge on the village streets, Siegfried feels he's descending into the unknown. The place is utterly unfamiliar to him. More than once he wonders who it is he's following and why.

They pass through an alleyway and he finds himself and the others looking through the back window of a dimly-lit house. Standing before an ornate wall mirror is a hooded man. Siegfried senses a vague hint of recognition coming through the fog in his brain.

The man raises his hands and lifts the hempen hood from his head. The face is still hidden but the outline of a beard is unmistakable.

'Matthias! I thought you said he'd esc —'

'This isn't the Matthias house,' Dieter whispers. 'Watch what happens next.'

'Whose house is —?'

'Just watch.'

Inside, turning from the mirror, the man slowly removes the false beard and looks towards the window, unaware of their presence. Siegfried staggers back, the truth blazing before his eyes.

'I can't believe it,' he chokes. 'It's ... it's ...'

NO WAY BACK

Each one waited, reluctant to be first to open his or her eyes. Anna wondered if this really was to be their final hour in the Grey Room. Greta, already quite sure that it was, tried to imagine what awaited them in Berlin. Dieter knew that his only option was to escape from Germany. In the real world he would be destined for some Special Home. He wondered, too, what lay ahead for Anna. Her whole race was despised by the Nazis. And who could tell what final solution to the 'problem' of Jews and cripples these people would dream up?

A more urgent concern was uppermost in their minds. Would Siegfried join them in their break for freedom? When they plucked up the courage, one by one, to look, the answer was as yet unclear. The fair-haired boy lay motionless between Dieter and Greta. They were so busy trying to wake him that they didn't hear Anna's breathless exclamation.

'The archway!'

'Siggy, wake up, Siggy. You're not dead any more .... I mean ... you never were.... Please, Siggy!'

There was no response to Dieter's calls.

'The archway!' Anna repeated.

'He changed the story, Siegfried,' Greta said. 'You were with us, you were talking to us just a minute ago in ...'

'Leiningen!'

They turned, not concealing their annoyance with Anna. 'It's gone. Leiningen is gone. The Leiningen archway is gone.'

In an agony of apprehension they looked towards the wall where Herr Gott's archway should be. Dieter was thinking how frail and ill Herr Gott had seemed that last time. A vast triple sigh of relief swept through the Grey Room as the last archway came into view. Dieter, however, sensed that the danger hadn't yet passed.

'If that archway disappears ... I mean, if anything happens to Herr Gott then we're trapped here ... forever.'

The message of his words was painfully clear to all of them. They had to leave right now — with or without Siegfried. They tried again to shake him from his final oblivion, but nothing worked. It was Greta who first faced the fact that it was over for him and that he wouldn't have wanted them to risk their futures by staying. In the end she and Anna had to drag Dieter away from Siegfried.

Then Greta knelt at Siegfried's side and said the only words that bore saying.

'Goodbye, Siegfried.'

Dieter fell to his knees and held his friend tightly with his one arm, just as he'd done in the story. This time there was no muffled protestation from Siegfried and no laughter.

'Bye ... S ... Siggy,' he whispered, and laid Siegfried back on the dusty floor of his eternal resting place.

Anna was beside Siegfried now. She bent over him and kissed his pallid cheek.

'We'll never forget you, Siegfried.'

They went sadly to Herr Gott's archway and together spun away into the old writer's room. The sight that greeted them there was one of utter chaos.

Among the colourless, patterned flowers of the worn carpet lay the black-uniformed Kroll. His close-shaven head was matted with blood. His breath came in short rattling gasps. Beside him was the blood-stained wreckage of a typewriter, its keys scattered about like lettered confetti. In his fist was the dagger-like letter-opener. How, they wondered amazedly, had the old man summoned the strength to overpower this brute?

All around them the contents of the room were strewn about — stale-smelling bedclothes, dozens of old shoes spotted with greeny-white mildew, leftover slabs of bread and sausage, a virtual snowfall of scrunched-up typing pages. They picked their way through the debris to the writing desk. A tidy bundle of stacked pages rested there, on top of which were Axel's *Prison Poems* and two handwritten notes.

Anna took the first note and began to read, the others peering over her shoulder at the ink-stained script. The first sentence brought back all the sadness of their parting with Siegfried. Anna read it aloud in a quavering voice.

'I hope that all of you are reading this note and that, by now, you have forgiven me my folly. I know you would have taken me from this city if that was what I'd wished. But it isn't, not any more.

'I am an old man. The time I have left on this earth is not long, my old bones have been telling me that for quite a while now. I have decided what I want to do with that time. A greater writer than I could ever be once said, "For evil to prevail, it only takes good men to remain silent." Perhaps I'm not a good man. But my silence is over. I must make my protest against Hitler and all those lackeys who will do anything, anything, in his name.

'Tonight, they are to burn more books on Unter Den Linden. They call it a celebration. I call it a sacrilege, a sin against God who is the Creator of all creators. I can't stop them, but I can raise my voice; and if I can touch the heart of even one of these firebrands then it will have been worthwhile. And even if I don't, I must take this course for the sake of my own peace of mind.

'As for the book, I have left it unfinished so that all of you can be free. I was on the point of burning this last Lingen Gang book when it occurred to me that it was the wrong thing to do. I thought, this book shows how a man — in this case a writer — can change his misguided ways and find his way to the truth. Why not preserve it for a future that is not as dark as this awful present? Why not bury it safely somewhere in the city, so that when this place is in ruins it may be found? And this city will one day be in ruins, nothing's surer. I believe with all my heart that when this book is read, along with poor Axel's poems, a light will be thrown on the dark past and a lesson learned for the future.

'It occurred to me too that the worst thing that can happen to a reader after ploughing through a book is to find that the last few pages are missing — the bit where you find out (even if you've already guessed) who the real culprit was and why they did what they did. So I've scribbled a few notes for the ending. Some day, perhaps, someone will finish it when you've all found your places in the world.

'About the money. Bring it to Herr Josef Ingelau at 15 Kammenstrasse. He'll get it to Romi.

'Finally, I want to thank you, Anna, Dieter, Greta and, of course, Siegfried, for saving my soul.

'Gott.'

The second note was headed, 'The Last of the Lingen Gang — Notes for an Ending'. There wasn't time to read it. Herr Gott had gone to make his stand but they couldn't leave him to the mercy of the book-burners.

'What about the book?' Anna asked as they went out by the open door of Herr Gott's room.

'We'll come back for it later,' Greta said, and they descended the long stairway to the damp night of Berlin.

Rain fell lightly but persistently. They stood looking left and right, wondering which way to go. A young fellow turned the corner onto the street and walked in their direction. In the mist-soaked light Dieter saw the fair hair, the broad shoulders — the light brown Hitler Youth uniform.

'Siggy!'

He ran towards the tall boy though Anna and Greta tried to hold him back. The Hitler Youth stopped in his tracks and suddenly Dieter stopped too. It wasn't Siegfried. The fellow looked at Dieter haughtily.

'Who do you think you're bawling at, cripple?'

Dieter remained calm. A fight, though he would certainly have relished it, was the last thing he needed now. Anna and Greta approached the pair hesitantly.

'We were wondering if you'd know where the book-burning is happening?' Greta asked.

The fellow's face brightened.

'Ah, yes, I've just brought some books there. Take a left, then left again and you're on Unter Den Linden. Turn right and follow the flames!'

'Thank you so much.'

The Hitler Youth raised his right arm in a salute.

'Heil Hitler!'

The girls reluctantly answered his salute. Dieter just stared at him. His patience was wearing thin. In the boy's face he saw the same blank-minded hate he'd seen in Siegfried's during the last chapters of the Lingen Gang book.

'Heil Hitler! What do you have to say?'

Waving his empty sleeve, Dieter moved within inches of the Hitler Youth.

'Heil My Bottom!' Dieter rasped, and skipped around the horrified boy.

When he'd regained his composure, the Hitler Youth made to leap at Dieter, but Anna's outstretched leg sent him tumbling and she and Greta bolted away to join the one-armed boy. Only when they'd reached the wide thoroughfare of Unter Den Linden were they sure they'd lost their pursuer. In any case, they were now well-hidden in the crowd surging towards the University where the burning ritual had begun. Luckily for them, the crowd was in a hurry so their own sense of urgency wasn't noticed.

Soon the shooting flames lit the skyline of trees before them and the faces of the rushing herd all around them. Eyes hypnotised by hate, dead lips drooling at the pleasure ahead, they seemed to Anna, Dieter and Greta just like the villagers of Leiningen, just as unreal, just as utterly mindless.

A cheer went up somewhere ahead of them, followed by a booming voice echoing out over the general mayhem of noise.

'And now it is my great pleasure to add another so-called masterpiece to the flames. Burn, Herr Hesse! You may have skulked away from us but soon you will burn like your books!'

A manic burst of applause thundered as if emerging from the earth. The devils in hell, Anna thought, are happy now.

At the massive bonfire they noticed how the crowd stood to one side, avoiding the smoke that was being blown eastward. They squeezed and harried their way to the front of the high podium where a tall man in black uniform yelled into a microphone. Hauptsturmführer Teufel!

He held yet another book aloft to the acclaim of the vast gathering.

'Sigmund Freud! Jew!'

He hurled the book down into the pyre below him. An instant later he had fallen to the floor of the platform. Herr Gott stood at the microphone, facing the bewildered spectators. He looked like an old drunk but he had never been more sober in his entire adult life.

'This is wrong,' he shouted. 'This is no way for a civilised people to behave. It's worse than wrong, it's madness. A great, a truly great German, yes, German writer, Heinrich Heine has said it. Said, "A country that burns its books is a mere step away from burning its people." You must stop, you ...'

Teufel's fist cracked into Herr Gott's jaw and sent him flying across the platform. The incensed Hauptsturmführer was having trouble loosening his Luger from its black leather holster. Dieter jumped the podium steps in fours and as Teufel whipped out his pistol he dived at him, hit him low and sent him swaying off balance. The shot meant for Herr Gott ripped into the trees beyond. The crowd scattered in all directions. Then the timber rail surrounding the platform gave way beneath Teufel's weight and he plunged outwards and down into the centre of the fire.

His screams were fearsome but he was beyond help. The flames were unapproachably hot and all his thrashing about served only to send him sinking deeper among them.

A force of SS and SA men charged through the panicking mob and within moments were surrounding the podium. Greta and Anna watched in horror as Dieter, trapped in that high place, leaned over Herr Gott, who was clutching grimly at his chest.

'Leave me,' Herr Gott moaned. 'Save yourself. Go, Siegfried, fly!'

It was pointless telling the dying old man he wasn't speaking to Siegfried. He wouldn't have heard anyway, he was so far gone. Dieter looked down below and saw the helplessness of his situation. His life in the real world was going to be a short one. Yet he felt quite calm.

'I'm afraid, my dear Herr Gott, I'm neither a bird nor an angel, so flying's out of the question! Herr Gott? Can you hear me?'

The old man had lost consciousness, but the pain in his chest which he'd sought to ease with his gnarled hands seemed still to shake him. A pair of gun-wielding SS men rushed up the steps, but just as the first one was about to put a foot on the platform he suddenly disappeared from sight. Dieter peered over the edge and saw that the steps had collapsed under their weight. All he could do was laugh and his laughter outraged the men below even more. Someone raised a gun and pointed it directly at Dieter.

'Don't shoot,' another ordered. 'We'll make them suffer a slow death! Tear down the platform!'

Three heavily-built Brownshirts gathered at each of the four timber struts that held the podium in place and began to heave the thing to and fro. Dieter rolled around, trying to get a grip on something to stop himself from falling.

A huge splintering sound rocked through him. The boards below him shuddered and he lost the hold he'd just got on Herr Gott. Without a cry or even a whimper, the old man fell all the way to the ground and was set upon by an angry knot of kicking, punching SS men. Anna and Greta could only look away, knowing there was nothing they could do to help him now.

The podium tottered dangerously over the flames and Dieter clung to two boards. Another loud crack of timber sent the whole structure spinning back from the fire. Anna and Greta ran around to the back of the podium, hoping that when it fell, as it soon would, it would fall not into the fire but back in their direction.

Again, Dieter found himself propelled forward to where the flames, hungry for more human flesh, danced. The rough plank he was clinging to suddenly gave way and he felt the heat singe his eyebrows as he hung, with nothing to hold on to, directly over the giant bonfire. He felt the plank move beneath him and rolled to the next one just before the first came loose and crashed down below.

'He's fallen in!'

The ranks of black and brown uniforms advanced as close as they might to the crackling blaze.

'Where is he? I can't see him!'

'I saw him. I saw him fall into the centre there!'

Meanwhile the podium, scorched with flame-licks, was careering backwards, and Dieter knew that although he'd never flown before there was always a first time. Seconds before the platform turned for its final descent into a molten oblivion, he drew in a deep breath and took off into the night. Behind him, the big timber gantry tumbled onto the fire and sent the SS and SA men ducking for cover.

For one moment of sheer elation Dieter thought that flight was truly possible. He flapped his arm, but he only spun downwards; if it hadn't been for Anna and Greta breaking his fall he would have hit the ground head first.

From tree to tree they ran, always watching to see if they'd been spotted. They made a break across the wide street and turned off Unter Den Linden. An unavoidable mistake. A shout of recognition rang in their ears as they made for Herr Gott's house.

At the front door they ducked in just as the mob entered the street from both ends, filling the narrow space like a flood. They were trapped. There was no way back. They ascended the stairs towards Herr Gott's blitzed-out room at the top of the building.

'If he's not dead yet,' Anna gasped breathlessly as they went up, 'we can go back into the Grey Room.'

'We might never get out of there again,' Greta panted.

'We're not going to get out of here alive, are we?' Dieter shouted above the hammering of their footsteps and those of the crowd giving chase. 'At least in the Grey Room they can't kill us.'

First to the top landing, Anna pushed open the door — and stopped so quickly that the others collided into her and they stumbled inside.

'Siegfried!' Anna cried. 'You're alive! I don't understand. Why didn't you wake when we did?'

'You lot were asleep,' Siegfried grinned. 'I was dead, remember? Takes a little longer to wake from the dead, don't you think?'

Siegfried dropped Herr Gott's handwritten notes where he'd found them just moments before. The stairwell outside was filling up with police and soldiers, all of them clamouring to be first to pounce on their prey.

'Get away from the door,' he yelled. 'Grab the desk. Come on!'

All four of them took hold of the writing desk and pulled it across to block the door. Siegfried looked around the room.

'The bed!'

They grappled with the unbelievably heavy antique until it too was in place on their barricade — just in time to withstand the first assault from outside. The force of three heaving shoulders on the door broke the square frame of the bed and one long iron beam fell inwards, just missing Greta's head.

Anna ran to the wall that once had been their passage to the Grey Room. It refused to yield. The Grey Room was no longer. The writers were dead. The Lingen Gang were free, delivered from their fictional existence — delivered to the mercy of a merciless mob.

She went to the window and threw it open. In dismay she looked across at a rooftop that was tantalisingly close and yet too distant to reach in one leap. Knowing that there was nothing more that could be added to the barricade, the others joined her. Dieter took one look outside and shook his head.

'It's three storeys down and God knows how many feet across.'

Anna broke away from the group and caught hold of the long piece of iron that had almost hit Greta. They saw what she was about as she lugged it to the window.

'It's not much more than three inches wide!'

'Do we have a choice, Siegfried?'

The juddering door, etched with widening fault-lines, was answer enough.

'Look, there's a broken slate near the bottom of that roof over there,' Greta said. 'If we can wedge it there it should hold.'

Soon the narrow iron trapeze was in place. Dieter volunteered to go first and climbed onto the windowsill. He put one foot on the beam and felt it sway. He wanted to turn back, make himself small in the corner of Herr Gott's room and hope they'd take pity on a poor cripple. But the very thought filled him with anger. The last thing he wanted was pity.

No! He would prove to himself and to the world that he was as brave and daring as anyone else. More than that, he'd give the others hope and make them believe in themselves too. There was only one way to do that. Make it look easy. In spite of fear, defying death, he'd make it seem like child's play. Which is precisely what he did, skipping across as if he were just a few inches off the ground below.

When he got to the other side he sat on the end of the beam to steady it for Anna. She crossed with the practised walk of an acrobat, full of confidence after seeing Dieter manage it so easily. Greta wasn't so lucky. Dieter was beginning to feel the pressure of holding the beam. She had taken only three steps when the iron tipped just a fraction. She stopped, paralysed with fear.

Dieter called out to her too loudly. 'You can do it. Just a few more steps!'

Greta's eyes were clamped shut and she wavered over the dark chasm. Anna spoke softly.

'Open your eyes, Greta. Open them now.'

Greta obeyed. She moved forward again. Dieter knew the beam was going off-balance again before Greta did.

'It's going! Get your hands on it, quick!'

In one sickening downward sweep the beam slipped from the window-ledge. Dieter and Anna held on at their end as Greta got a grip on the cold iron with one hand and then with both. She hung over the huge drop, telling herself, convincing herself that she wasn't too heavy for her two friends to hold.

Anna and Dieter hauled the beam upwards and when Greta appeared Anna grasped her hand. Greta's weight dragged her down. Dieter let go of the beam and with an almighty tug of his one arm brought both of them to safety. Down below, the iron beam clattered onto the concrete yard.

Back at the window, Siegfried heard the ringing crash above the din of the axe splitting the door to Herr Gott's room. In his hands he held the Lingen Gang book, the notes and poems, all bundled into an old pillowcase. He knotted the open end of the makeshift bag.

'Catch this!'

He flung the pillowcase into Anna's arms.

'Get another of those bed-irons!' Dieter roared.

Siegfried looked behind. The door was in bits. The men in black and brown were pushing back the barricade. He could see the whites of their glaring eyes.

'Too late. I'll have to jump.'

The writing desk shot across the floor. The icy glint of a pistol was the last thing Siegfried saw before he took his chance and sprang from the windowsill.

Perhaps there was still some of the angel in him, still some trace of the strange powers that had brought him from the invented world of Leiningen to the real world and back so many times. Whatever it was, he made the jump to the next rooftop. As soon as his hands touched those slates he knew with absolute certainty that he'd never be capable of such a superhuman feat again.

'What are we waiting for? Let's clear out of here!'

They clambered over the ridge of the roof and down the opposite side. Shots pierced the sky above them but they were out of sight of the gunmen. All along the sloping avenue of roofs they searched for a way to get to ground level. They reached a two-storey house and were relieved to see a series of stores and sheds behind it, descending like giant stairs. From the last low building they were able to jump the final six feet into a lane lit only by the glow from the distant flames on Unter Den Linden.

Here they listened for the roar of the crowd as they took time to catch their breaths. There was nothing to hear but the odd passing car and the squeal of cats on the prowl. They sat against the wall of the lane. For all their relief, a sense of great sadness prevailed amongst them. It wasn't only the chase that was over, or their lives in Leiningen and in the Grey Room. Each of them knew, in their different ways, that their life together was over.

'We'll have to split up,' Siegfried said. 'It's our only chance. We have to find our way out of Berlin.'

'If we went in pairs, maybe,' Dieter suggested without any great conviction.

Greta shook her head.

'There are too many people who saw us tonight. If they spot one of us they mightn't be sure, but if they recognise two faces together they'll be certain.'

There was no further argument on the matter. None of them wanted to spoil their last moments together.

'We have a promise to keep for Herr Gott. The money. I'll get it.'

'But you can't do it on your own, Siggy.'

'He brought me back to life. Let me repay him.'

'I'll take the book,' Anna said, 'and bury it like he asked.'

What more was there to say? Nothing. They smiled at one another and it seemed too small and meaningless a gesture to express what they felt.

Siegfried turned and walked into the shadowless depths of the lane. Soon the others, too, had gone their separate ways.

At the bank clerk's empty flat, Siegfried was forced to put his shoulder to the door to break in. On the floor below a curious old woman came out on the landing.

'What are you doing up there?'

Siegfried managed to conceal his fright behind a superior look.

'Get back inside, woman. Herr Gier is under investigation.'

The old woman's eyes bulged open.

'Really? What's he been up to?'

'The man's a thief. Now go back to your room this instant. And not a word to anyone, right?'

The stolen money awaited Siegfried on Herr Gier's table.

The Hitler Youth uniform proved to be Siegfried's guarantee of safety as he searched for Kammenstrasse. At No. 15, Herr Ingelau was at first unwilling to take the stuffed envelope of money. He suspected anyone who wore a uniform. The overwhelming events of this night were taking their toll on Siegfried. He lost patience with the man's suspicious reaction to him.

'Just give it to Romi. It was Herr Gott's last wish.'

'You mean he's ...'

'Give it to her. Tell her ... tell her that her father was a good man.'

Herr Ingelau took the envelope.

'I don't trust that uniform but I can trust your face. What's your name, young man?'

'My name? I don't have one. Maybe tomorrow I'll find one.'

Down by the southern outskirts of Berlin, Anna, still bearing her little parcel, came upon a deserted building site. A scheme of grand houses was half-completed there. Among the eerily quiet rooms she found what she was looking for, and some other bits and pieces she hadn't realised she'd need until they came to hand.

With the spade she'd found she began to dig behind one of the houses where, she supposed, a lawn would one day be sown. Her soft hands blistered quickly but she carried on without a pause until the hole was deep enough. Then she folded a wide strip of lead around the pillowcase, and with a hammer she beat the edges together so that the lead formed a little casket. Unprotected, the pillowcase and its contents might have rotted in a matter of weeks. Now the book, notes and poems would survive for years. With a long rusty nail she scraped a message on the lead and retraced it until her fingers were raw. The message said simply: 'Read this book. 1934.'

Anna placed the casket in the damp earth and began to shovel the clay over it. A curiously dizzy sensation overcame her and with each falling spadeful of clay her mind grew more and more numb. It was the numbness of forgetting. All her memories were vanishing, all the adventures, the good and the bad, the Grey Room days, the faces of Axel and Herr Gott and Teufel, the names and faces of the other Lingen Gang members. And finally, with the last clump of earth, her own name left her, along with every trace of her past.

At the same moment Siegfried, Greta and Dieter lost every last memory they had.

It was the end. It was the beginning.

THE LAST
OF THE
LINGEN GANG

(NOTES FOR AN ENDING)

1. Herr Hempel is, of course, the villain of the piece — but the real villain is Adolf Hitler.

2. Why did Herr Hempel do what he did? Because tyrants like Hitler (and, in his own small way, Hempel) can only gain power and cling to it in a climate of fear. The people must be afraid so that the tyrant can say 'I will protect you'. Therefore he must find something, someone for people to fear. Hitler has chosen the Jews. They are wicked, evil, greedy, he rants. They have tried to destroy our country, have tried to bleed it to death. Look at all the rich, fat Jews, he says, where did their money come from? Theft, moneylending, the black market — where else! His message is: if we don't destroy them, they will destroy us.

And 'cripples' too. All handicapped people are a burden on society. Money spent on them is wasted and the more money we waste, the greater the chance that we will starve. Is that what you want, the tyrant cries? You want to die of hunger or live a hand-to-mouth existence like some Russian peasant because we throw our hard-earned money away on cripples?

3. Men like Hempel in every town and village bring this message to the people, and in each town and village a scapegoat must be found. Herr Hempel chose Matthias and tried to make him seem like a terrorist. Bringing in henchmen from outside who wouldn't be recognised he almost succeeded.

4. Because Hempel controls everything in the village, including the police, the Gang know he won't be arrested. They must keep his secret or be arrested themselves. But they know he'll pay the price in the end, however long it takes.

5. The Lingen Gang becomes a secret society dedicated to resisting the onslaught of Nazism. Siegfried will remain in the Hitler Youth, Greta in the League of German Girls, and both will try at every opportunity to sabotage their activities. It is Dieter who convinces them they must do this. As for himself, he reckons it is time he moved on. He knows that Hempel plans to consign him to a Special Home and he has no intention of waiting around for that to happen.

EPILOGUE

In the years following those events of May 1934, Adolf Hitler's dream of a great German Empire flourished. In time, Germany was no longer a big enough place to satisfy the needs of the Nazis. Its borders were pushed out and this drive to expansion inevitably led to world war in 1939. Until 1942, gain followed gain; but in the summer and autumn of that year the tide slowly began to turn.

World War II ended in defeat for Germany in 1945, but not before the last bastion of Hitler's empire, the city of Berlin, was torn stone from stone and transformed into a smoky grey moonscape. Among these ruins, Adolf Hitler cursed the weakness and unworthiness of the German people and turned a gun on himself.

But Germany's misery hadn't yet ended, and nowhere was this misery more evident than in Berlin. Soon it was to become a divided city. The Allied Powers, Britain, France and America, controlled the western side. The Russians controlled the east. In 1962 this division was cemented with the erection of the Berlin Wall. Twenty-seven years were to pass before this edifice was dismantled by a new generation of Germans.

On an unforgettable night in October of 1989, the German people streamed through the Berlin Wall's narrow checkpoints and danced and cried in the streets. Before long, the bulldozers began to move in and the demolition of the Wall commenced.

That is where the end of this story begins.

~

The following news item was carried first in the German daily, *Der Spiegel*, and next day in newspapers around the world.

BERLIN, 18th DECEMBER

An extraordinary literary find has been made by workers engaged in the dismantling of the Berlin Wall on the southern side of the city. A home-made lead casket, bearing the inscription 'Read this book. 1934', was found to contain the typescript of an unfinished novel for young people entitled The Last of the Lingen Gang. *Explanatory notes for a suggested ending were also included.*

Literary experts are puzzled by the fact that the book does not appear to have been solely the work of Axel Hoffen, the original creator of the Lingen Gang series. This series of adventures was enormously popular in the early 30s but had, until now, been forgotten. The signature on the explanatory notes is that of Hans Gott, a prominent writer in the early part of this century whose books are still studied in universities. The mystery deepened when a set of poems by Axel Hoffen was discovered among the pages of the typescript.

The book is now thought to have been a collaboration between the two men, though no evidence of their ever meeting is available. The fact that both men died in 1934 at the hands of the SS may, in time, provide further clues as to the origins of this book.

Speaking from his home in New York, the publisher Josef Stieglitz, whose grandfather fled Germany in 1934, had no doubt as to the book's significance.

He stated, 'I intend to publish it, along with the poems of Axel Hoffen, as an act of gratitude to two writers who made the ultimate sacrifice for their beliefs.'

~

In Tel Aviv, the sun is a golden ball slowly descending nightwards. A grey-haired woman, her face still as darkly pretty as when she was a girl, prays in the sacred Hebrew with her grandchildren. She has good reason to thank her God, for she has found purpose and fulfilment in her long life, despite the bitter memories of Teresenstadt and Dachau concentration camps. Tonight she has even greater reason to give thanks.

All her life, even after her marriage to a kind man who died too young, even after the birth of her children, there has been an emptiness deep inside her. There are questions she has never found answers to. Why can't I remember my early years? Why can't I remember my parents or whether I had brothers or sisters or friends? Where did I live? Where did I come from?

Many survivors of the death camps recall little or nothing of those horrendous days, but she remembers every detail of them. So why can she not remember what went before?

In spite of this she's got on with her life, hoping that one day the memories will return. But they never have.

Today she read this news from Berlin, the story of a buried book. Though she doesn't recognise any of the names — Axel Hoffen, Hans Gott, the Lingen Gang — she feels a sense of peace. She accepts that some questions can never be answered and resolves never to ask them again. She has never known such undiminished happiness, and she savours it. And there is so much to do with her new-found serenity, so many people to tell in her chosen way.

~

Snow covers the town of Hurley in upstate New York. Despite the fact that later he'll have to dig a path from his front door one-handed with a shovel, this elderly but sprightly man isn't at all concerned. A great weight has been lifted from his mind. He sits opposite his wife of forty years, before the glow of a warm fire. He browses through the piece in the *New York Times* once again.

Berlin! It's been fifty-five years since he escaped that city and sneaked on board the S.S. Bremen bound for the sanctuary of America.

'What's got into you?' his wife asks cheerily. 'You're like a sly old cat who's stolen the cream. Hatching another plot, are you?'

He shakes his head, bewildered and elated.

'I don't know. Something I read here. It means nothing and it means everything. I feel so ... so happy ... so contented.'

She has grown used to his riddling way of talking. This, she supposes, is how people in his line of work have always talked, their minds always seeming to be in at least two places at the same time.

'When was the last time I told you I loved you?' he asks, leaning forward and extending his one arm towards her.

'When you asked me to make coffee for you this morning, I believe. Go make it yourself!'

'Yeah, why don't I? And hey, if I'm the sly old cat like you say, how'd you like some of my stolen cream in your coffee?'

~

It's raining, as it often does in Ireland, but she's never thought less of the place for its dampness. She has known happy times in this small but elegantly-furnished cottage in the village of Holycross. She has many friends who often call, but tonight she's alone and this doesn't bother her. She's always chosen to live this way. The vague loneliness that has always possessed her has nothing to do with her independent style of living. It has to do with the missing years of her early life. Or rather, it *had* to do with that huge gap in her memory, until today.

The article in today's paper repeats itself in her mind as she rests on the mountain of pillows she favours. She's read it so often she knows it by heart. She knows it as well as she knows the words of the beautiful songs she listens to every night before she sleeps. She's listening to them now. The poems of Friedrich Ruckert set to music by Mahler, a Jewish composer whose work was frowned upon by the Nazis.

She too has found peace in some inexplicable way. She no longer feels lonely, only glad to have met so many decent and good people along the hazardous journey to this small cottage. The years of menial work, of waitressing, floor-scrubbing and later picking among the debris of battered Berlin for scraps to eat, rags to wear, have taught her what it is to be poor.

A chance meeting with an Irish officer in the British Army, who was kind and light-hearted and who gave her her first secretarial job, decided her on seeing his country some time. Eventually in 1957 she got to Ireland. The officer was long married to the redheaded girl whose photo he'd shown her back in Berlin, but with his help she began to achieve success in the work that was the real love of her life. Now she knows what it is like to be, if not rich, then comfortably off. But money couldn't buy what she's gained tonight.

For months now the crippling arthritis has slowed her down, the pain distracting her from her work. She had begun to believe that her work was done. She is old, after all. How old, she has no clear idea. Time she rested, she thought. But there would be no rest with that eternal mystery of an unremembered childhood hanging over her.

As soon as she read the article for the first time the pain eased. With every re-reading, and now with every recitation of those newspaper words, it lessened more. Her mind cleared. She knows better than most that it's useless to wonder where good fortune comes from. Better to grasp it and go on, always go on.

She closes her eyes and listens to the song ending, singing softly those last lines that always accompany her to the sanctuary of sleep.

'Ich leb' allein....

I live alone in my own heaven,

In my love, in my song.'

~

The crisp night air of Hamburg is filled with the twinkling promise of Christmas. A small fair-haired boy muffled up to the ears runs excitedly ahead of his parents towards the big toy-shop window.

'Only a week to go,' the six-year-old reminds them. 'I can't wait!'

Face pressed against the glass, he peers in at the vast array of toys, each more tempting than the next. His list for Sankt Nikolaus is written and in the post. He looks closer to see if he can spot the toys he's asked for.

'There's my Batmobile! Wow, it's brilliant!'

His parents catch up with him and stand behind him. His mother beams happily at the boy's excitement. His father smiles too, but there is sadness in his eyes. He wishes he were a child again, if only for a day, even an hour. For his son's sake he pushes these thoughts to the back of his mind.

'Look over there. Isn't that the Power Ranger, the blue one, you want?'

But the boy doesn't answer. His head isn't bobbing around in search of his chosen delights any more. Only now does his father notice that in one corner of the window is a display of toys from long ago. An old-fashioned spinning top, complete with the stick and string to spin it; building blocks, their edges worn from use, their brick patterns faded; an enormous doll's-house with perfectly proportioned furniture and fittings; a Red Indian Chief's long, trailing head-dress; a loose-stringed bow with a quiver of rubber-topped arrows. And a dog-eared old paperback book, the colours of its cover gone grey with time.

'See the boy on the book. He looks just like you, Daddy!'

'Listen here, I'm old but I'm not that old!'

'Then it's ... I know ... it's Grandad! I said it, I said he didn't die. See, Daddy? He went into that book! I want it, Daddy, I don't care about the other things. I want that book, Daddy!'

'Maybe you're right. Books were his life, weren't they?'

The boy's mother kneels down beside him and tries to explain.

'That book isn't for sale. And besides, you're not ready for all those big words just yet.'

He turns his face from the window and gives her one of those looks young children are so good at — a look that tells you you're the cruellest person in the world and asks how you could hurt a small child like this.

His father stares at the book cover. *The Adventures of the Lingen Gang*. Four happy faces, one remarkably like that old photo of his father as a young man. The one he keeps in his wallet. What was it his father said on that morning, just three months before, when he passed away?

'I've had every reason to be happy in my life,' he remembers the old man whispering. 'A good wife, a good son. Even those years I spent in prison for refusing to follow orders weren't all bad. But one thing I never had was a childhood. I did my best to give you a happy childhood and I know you'll do the same for your son.'

The man bends down, picks up the small boy and holds him close.

'You shall have the book,' he promises. 'No matter what it costs I'll buy it for you, Siegfried.'

~

In Hurley, New York, it is ten o'clock at night and the snow is bright under the moon.

In Holycross it is three in the morning and the wind stirs the trees.

In Tel Aviv it is seven and the sky is red with the glow of dawn.

Three writers, thousands of miles apart, share the same dream. They are in Leiningen. Young again, they lie in the long grass of a sloping field. Above them is Lingen Peak; below, the ruins of the old Castle. The Lingen Gang is meeting again and this time it's Siegfried who's late. None of them speaks because they're afraid to say that he might not come. They don't understand why he shouldn't. It's just a feeling, but it hangs heavily in the air about them.

They wait, and their waiting becomes a cloud shrouding the sun. A mountain breeze whips the grass into a frenzied lashing. All is grey.

They rise to leave. The wind stops. The cloud passes. A figure appears on the ancient battlements below.

'Anna, Dieter, Greta!' Siegfried calls, and leaps from the heights.

They move, all four, through eternal fields, telling each other the stories of their lives, the stories they have each written and read and heard and imagined. Stories enough to fill eternity.

And this story is only one of them.

CAVAN COUNTY LIBRARY

THE PRISON POEMS
OF AXEL HOFFEN

IN DARKNESS

I was singing night songs
In the morning of my youth.
I didn't know what night was
But now I know the truth.

I had the key to happiness
Being young with games to play
But I sat at a writing desk
And locked the key away.

I fumbled in the darkness
And racked my tired brain
But not until I knew real fear
Did I real wisdom gain.

That man's a simple creature
Is all there is to say.
By day he dreams of heavenly night,
By night he dreams of day.

THE DEVIL

The devil came knocking upon my door.
I guessed what he was coming for.
His coat was black and black his mood;
A cold black insect — I, his food.

I thought he'd come to take my life.
I waited for the silver knife.
But what he wanted was my mind
To harden the hearts of humankind.

Wanting to live in spite of fear
I almost said what he wished to hear
But something touched me like a hand
And I refused his dark command.

I MADE A BOY

I made a boy inside my mind.
I gave him friends, I gave him
strength.
I made him true and kind.

I made a village, Leiningen,
With narrow streets, a place complete
With thrills and spills — but then

The boy was taken from my mind
And made to follow that mad ruffian,
The Beast of all mankind.

But he escaped from the black-dressed
men
And now he fights for his real life
Beyond my dried-up pen.

ALL MY DREAMS COME TRUE

Madness came into my prison cell.
Fear paved the way
For promises of pain will always tell
The mind to run away.

I heard the voice right by my ear
Repeat maddeningly,
'I'm here, I'm here, Siegfried is here'
And thought it utter fantasy.

But then I knew him to be real,
The one I made,
And sadness made my heart to feel
He'd too soon fade.

It seemed my freedom gone forever,
His must be too —
No! Though I am just a mere creator,
All my dreams come true!

ANGELS WITHOUT WINGS

What happens when the heavenly air
Is darkened by the devils?
Where do the good and just go, where?
What happens to the angels?

They roam the earth and cleanse the hearts
Of paupers and of kings.
But at what cost do they play their parts,
These angels without wings?

They'll make a heaven of this earth
A little more each day,
Reminding us of our self-worth —
But what's the price they pay?

To make a paradise so great
From human, low beginnings
They'll wander far from Heaven's gate,
These angels without wings.

Also from Award-Winning
MARK O'SULLIVAN

White Lies

A ROLLER-COASTER STORY OF REAL LOVE

For Nance, it begins with the photo she finds in her
adoptive mother's room –
a photo of herself as a black baby,
with the parents she has never known.

For OD, it begins with his father's decision
to buy a trumpet –
and with Mick Moran's strange visit to the Town Park
building site where OD works.

Both of them need to know the truth before their lives –
and their relationship – can go on.

But as their search continues, they discover that
everybody has secrets –
and that the truth is never as simple as it seems.

ISBN 0-86327-591-5

More than a Match

It is the summer of 1948. Reigning tennis champ
Lida Hendel has a temper to match her serve.
When sixteen-year-old Ginny Stannix turns up on the
scene, Lida meets her toughest challenge yet.
Intrigue, slander and rumours of shameful secrets reach
breaking point as the final looms large.
ISBN 0-86327-496-X

Wash-Basin Street Blues:
Nora in New York

The omens are foreboding. Whose is the frightening face
pressed against the window?
What is the metallic clanging sound disturbing
Nora's dreams?
On its own or as a sequel to *Melody for Nora*,
this novel is an action-packed read.
ISBN 0-86327-467-6

Melody for Nora:
One Girl's Story in the Civil War

Winner of the Eilís Dillon Memorial Award 1995
Nominated for the 1995 Bisto Book of the Year Award
'Gripping.' *Irish Times*
ISBN 0-86327-425-0